THE SPANISH FARM

R. H. Mottram

With a Preface by

John Galsworthy

Simon Publications

2001

Library of Congress Control Number:
24017905

ISBN: 1-931313-82-2

Distributed by Ingram Book Company

Printed by Lightning Source Inc. La
Vergne, TN

Published by Simon Publications, P.O. Box
321, Safety Harbor, FL 34695

CONTENTS

*

PREFACE

By John Galsworthy

"THE Spanish Farm" attracts a preface because it exhibits a new form, distinct even in this experimental epoch ; and because one has not before met with such a good realization of French character by an Englishman, unless Renée, in " Beauchamp's Career," be excepted.

For four years and three months the British Army was in France, many thousands of educated Englishmen were in touch with French character, and, so far as I know, Madeleine in this book is the only full, solid, intimate piece of French characterization which has resulted from that long and varied contact. Madeleine is amazingly lifelike. I suspect her to be a composite creation rather than drawn directly from one living prototype ; however that may be, there she is, an individual Frenchwoman of the North, firm as ever stood on excellent legs—no compromise about her outlines, nothing fluffy and nothing sketchy in her portrait from beginning to end. She imposes herself, page by page, with her tenacity, her clear knowledge of what she wants, her determined way of getting it, her quick blood, her business capacity, and once more, her tenacity—the tenacity which has kept the Spanish farm in her family since the days of Alva. Besides being a warm-

PREFACE

blooded, efficient, decisive human being, with a wonderful eye to the main chance, she is evidence on French character extremely valuable to those among us who really want to understand the French.

And the minor portraits, of her lover Georges, and his old parents, of her father, her sister, and the housekeeper at the château, with the young English officer as foil, fill in a convincing picture of French life and atmosphere in the war zone.

I suppose you would call this a war book, but it is unlike any other war book that I, at least, have met with. Its defined and realized scope, its fidelity and entire freedom from meretricity make it a singularly individual piece of work.

And that brings me to its form—the chief reason for this short preface. "The Spanish Farm" is not precisely a novel, and it is not altogether a chronicle ; and here the interest comes in—quite clearly the author did not mean it to be a novel, and fail ; nor did he mean it to be a chronicle, and fail. In other words, he was guided by mood and subject-matter into discovery of a new vehicle of expression—going straight ahead with that bold directness which guarantees originality. Easy enough to find fault with "The Spanish Farm" if you judge it strictly as a novel, or strictly as a chronicle, in fact if you take it strictly for what it is not—that pet weakness of hasty criticism. The book has its imperfections—what book has not ?—but I do not think the serious critic

PREFACE

can miss the peculiar unforced feeling of novelty
its form has given me. You do not put it down
saying : " I see perfectly what form the fellow
was trying for, but he didn't bring it off." You
put it down thinking : " The fellow didn't seem
to be trying for any form, but he did bring it off."

We know the self-conscious chronicle in fiction,
and its—as a rule—artificial effect. " The Spanish Farm " is as far from that as it is from the
dramatic novel. It just goes its own way, and
quietly defeats the search for parallels. One
might perhaps best call it highly humanized history. It is, anyway, a very interesting book, with
a just—if unexpected—title, for one never loses
consciousness of Madeleine's home, that solid old
farmstead of French Flanders, named in the
Spanish wars of centuries ago, and still in being,
after the greatest war of all time.

JOHN GALSWORTHY,

1924

PART I

LA PATRIE EST EN DANGER

PART I

La Patrie est en danger

A FARMER stood watching a battalion of infantry filing into his pasture. A queerer mixture of humanity could not have been imagined. The farmer wore a Dutch cap, spoke Flemish by preference, but could only write French. His farm was called Ferme l'Espagnole —The Spanish Farm—and stood on French soil. The soldiers were the usual English mixture— semi-skilled townsmen, a number of agricultural and other labourers, fewer still of seafaring and waterside folk, and a sprinkling of miners and shepherds, with one or two regulars.

The farmer, Mr. Vanderlynden, Jerome, described in the Communal records as a Cultivator, sixty-five years of age, watching his rich grass being tramped to liquid mud under the heavy boots of the incoming files, and the shifting of foot-weary men as they halted in close column, platoon by platoon, made no protest. This was not merely because under the French law he was bound to submit to the needs of the troops, but also because, after twelve months' experience, he had discovered that there were compensations attached to the billeting and encampment of English. They paid—so much per officer or man—not always accurately, but promptly always, and what would you more in war-time? The

3

THE SPANISH FARM

Spanish Farm was less than twenty kilometres from the " Front," the actual trenches, whose ground-shaking gun-rumble was always to be heard, whose scouting aeroplanes were visible and audible all day, whose endless flicker of star shells made green the eastern horizon all night. The realities of the situation were ever present to Mr. Jerome Vanderlynden, who besides could remember a far worse war, that of 1870. Moreover, the first troops passing that way in the far-off days of 1914 had been French, and had wanted twice as much attention, and had never paid, had even threatened him when he suggested it.

*　　　*　　　*　　　*

Standing with his great knotted earthy fists hanging by his side, as the khaki stream poured and poured through the wide-set gate, he passed in review the innumerable units or detachments that had billeted in the Spanish Farm or encamped in its pastures. Uncritical, almost unreasoning, the old peasant was far from being able to define the difference he had felt when the first English arrived. He had heard tell of them, read of them in the paper, but was far from imagining what they might have been like, having no data to go on and no power of imagination. He had been coming in from getting up the last of the potato crop of 1914 when he had found flat-capped, mud-coloured horsemen at his gate. Sure that they were Germans (the Uhlans had been as near as

4

Hazebrouck only a few weeks before), he hastily tied the old white horse in the tombereau, and had gone forward cap in hand. But his daughter Madeleine had already met the soldiers at the gate. A widower for many years, Jerome Vanderlynden's house was kept by his youngest child, this Madeleine, now in her twentieth year. To say that he believed in her does not do justice to his feelings. She had been the baby of the family, had had a better education than he or his sons, at a convent in St. Omer ; added to all this, plus her woman's prestige, was the fact that she inherited (from heaven knows where !) a masterful strain. What she said (and she was not lavish of words) was attended to. Whether it were education, inspiration, or more probably an appreciation beyond the powers of her father, that told her that English cavalry officers would agree with her, it is certain that she started with those first squadrons of the Cavalry Division a sort of understanding that she would never have attempted with French troops. They paid her liberally and treated her respectfully, probably confusing her in their minds with English farmers' wives to whom they were in the habit of paying for hunt damage. They had money—officers and men wanted to supplement their rations and the horses' forage. Madeleine had eggs, coffee, soft bread, beer, fried potatoes, beans, oats. She could and did wash collars and shirts better than the average soldier servant. It took her some time to understand that every English officer required many gallons of water to wash in, at least once a day. But once she had grasped that too, she attended to it, at a small charge.

*　　*　　*　　*

And now it was October, 1915 ; more troops than ever, especially infantry, were in the Commune, and an interpreter had warned Jerome Vanderlynden that he would have a whole battalion in the farm. He made no remark, but Madeleine had asked several questions. More awake mentally than her father, it had not escaped her close reading of the paper that a new sort of English troops were coming to France. They were described indifferently as " Territorials " and as " New Army " or " Kitchener's Army," and neither Madeleine nor indeed the newspapers of the Department du Nord knew of any difference between them and the Territoriaux of the French system. Madeleine put them down as second-line troops and stored the fact in her vigilant mind.

She came and stood beside her father, as the 10th Battalion Easthamptonshire Regiment broke up and moved off to its billets. Two of the sadly depleted companies went to adjacent farms, two remained on the premises. The officers— of whom only twelve had survived the Battle of Loos—were busy with non-coms., going through nominal rolls, lists of missing men or damaged

6

equipment, trying to disentangle some sort of parade state and indent for replacements.

Madeleine did not bother about them. She said to her father : " I am going to find the Quarta-mastere ! "

She found him, standing amid his stores in the hop-press, and knew him by his grey hair and white-red-white ribbon. She had long ago inquired and found out that this rank in the English Army were chosen from among the old soldiers, and were quickest at getting to business. It had been explained to her that the white-red-white ribbon was for length of good conduct, and secretly tolerant of men's foibles as of a child's, she stored this fact also, for identification purposes.

In this instance the Mess President having been killed, the old ranker, Lieutenant and Quartermaster John Adams, was acting Mess President, and doing nearly every other duty in the disorganization and readjustment that followed the tragic bungle of the New Army's first offensive.

He greeted her with his professional aplomb : " Good day, Maddam, dinner for twelve officers ; compris, douze ! " He held up the fingers of both hands and then two fingers separately.

" All right ! " returned Madeleine in English. " Where are their rations ? "

He replied, " Ah, you're sharp ! " and called to his storekeeper, " Jermyn, officers' rations

7

to Maddam and tell the mess cook ! " He went on to bargain for other things—beds for the Colonel, the Adjutant and himself—and in the course of the argument Madeleine informed him that according to General Routine Orders there was to be no smoking in the barns and no insanitary practices, that all gates must be kept closed, and no movables removed. Handing him her price list, she withdrew to her long coffin-shaped stove in the brick-floored kitchen.

*   *   *   *

Dusk settled down on the Spanish Farm—autumn dusk—with swathed mists on the small flat chocolate-coloured fields, richest and best tilled in the world—now bare of crops. The brilliant colours of the last hop-leaves and of the regular rows of elms that bordered each pasture were hidden, but the tops of the trees towered above the mist-line into that wide blue vault that the old painters loved, nowhere wider than in the Flemish plain. The Spanish Farm stood on the almost imperceptible southern slope of the sandy ridge that divides in some degree the valley of the Yser from that of the Lys, whose flat meadows lay spread out, almost from Aire to the factory smoke of Armentières, at a slightly lower level to the south. Northward, behind the house, the ground rose very gradually in fertile field and elm-encircled pasture. Westward, black against the last glow of the sunset, two little 'planes droned

their way from the aerodromes round St. Omer
toward the eastern horizon where the evening
" hate " was toned down by the distance to the
low boom of " heavies," the sharper note of the
field-guns, the whip-lash crack of rifles and
machine-guns, and the flatter squashed-out reports
of mortars and grenades.

The house itself was a single-storied building
of immensely thick walls of red brick—much as
the settlers under Alva had left it three hundred
years before—except for enlargement of windows
and re-thatching—though the existing thatch
was so old that wallflowers tasselled its ridge from
one octagonal spoke-tiled chimney-stack to the
other. Originally a simple block with door in
the middle, outbuildings had been added at each
end, giving it the form of an unfinished quad-
rangle, the gap toward the south, enclosing the
great steaming midden of golden dung. Completely surrounded by a deep wide moat, access to
it was only possible by a brick bridge on the
southern side, guarded by a twenty-foot extin-
guisher-roofed " shot " tower, whose loopholed
bulk now served for tool shed below and pigeon-
loft above.

Further outbuildings stood outside the moat,
a few to the north in the smaller pasture behind
the house, but a long broad range of cowshed,
stable, and hop-press stretched into the ten-acre
" home " or " manor " pasture.

Never, since Alva last marched that way, had

the old semi-fortress been so packed with humanity. Two companies, which even at their present weakness must have numbered over three hundred men, were getting rid of their arms and equipment and filing round to the north pasture where the cookers flared and smoked, and the cooks, demoniac in their blackened faces and clothes, ladled out that standard compost that, at any time before nine in the morning was denominated "coffee," at any hour before or after noon "soup," until the end of the day, when, as a last effort, it became "tea." Derisive shouts of "Gyp-oh !" intended to convey that it was accepted for what it was— yesterday's bacon grease, hot water and dust from the floor of a lorry—greeted it, as it splashed into the tendered mess-tins of the jostling crowd.

*   *   *   *

Within the house, in the westward of the two principal rooms, Madeleine, with Berthe, most useful of the Belgian refugees about the place, had got her stove nearly red hot, and was silently, deftly handling her pots and dishes, while the mess cooks unpacked the enamelled plates and cups and carried them through to the other room where the table was being set by the simple process of spreading sheets of newspapers upon it and arranging the drinking-cups, knives and forks thereon. Bread being cut, there only remained for "Maddam," as they called Madeleine, to say that all was ready, so that the brass shell-case in

the passage could be used as a gong. The
Colonel appeared, and the Adjutant, both regular
soldiers, masking whatever they felt under professional passivity. There were no other senior
officers ; the only surviving Major was with a
captainless outlying company. The two companies in the farm were commanded by lieuten-
ants. The junior officers were all Kitchener
enlistments. Some of them had hoped to spend
that night in Lille.

The conversation was not so brilliant as the
meal. In many a worse billet, the Easthamptons
looked back to their night at Spanish Farm.
Every one was dog tired and bitterly depressed.
The Colonel only sat the length of one cigarette.
Adams took his food in his " bunk." The junior
officers clattered up the narrow candle-lit stair
into the loft where two of them had a bedstead
and two others the floor. The Adjutant was left
collating facts and figures, with the Doctor, who
was going through his stores. To them came
the runner from the guard-room (improvised in a
tent at the brick-pillared gate of the pasture).

" Reinforcement officers, sir ! "

There entered two rather bewildered young
men who had passed during the previous forty-
eight hours through every emotion from a desperate fear that the " victory " of Loos would end
the war without their firing a shot, to sheer annoyance at being dumped at a railhead and told to
find a battalion in the dark. They had lost every-

thing they had except what they carried on them, and were desperately hungry.

The Adjutant surprised even himself at the cordial greeting he gave the two strangers—untried officers from a reserve battalion he had never seen. He knew nothing of their history or capabilities, but the sense of more people behind, coming up to fill the gaps, warmed even the professional soldier's trained indifference. He got up, and went to the door of the kitchen, calling for " Maddam " and repeating " Mangay " in a loud voice to indicate that further refreshment was required.

Madeleine had just finished, with Berthe, the washing and cleaning up of her cooking utensils, and was about to go to bed in her little single bedroom that looked out over the northern pasture. She was just as inclined to cook another meal as a person may be, who has already worked eighteen hours and expects to rise at half-past five in the morning. Nor was there anything in the stare of the shorter, fair-haired new arrival, with his stolid silence, to encourage her. But the taller and darker of the two asked her in fair French if she could manage an omelet and some coffee. They regretted deranging her, but had the hunger of a wolf and had not eaten since the morning. Whether it was being addressed in her own tongue, or the fact that the young officer had hit on the things that lay next her hand and would not take five minutes, or whether it was something in the voice, Madeleine acquiesced politely, and set about providing what was asked.

The Adjutant stared. He was not accustomed to interpolations in foreign tongues in his orders. But this young officer was so obviously unconscious of offence, and the interference so opportune, that there was nothing to be said. He talked to the new-comers as they supped, and, apologizing for having to put them in the little ground-floor room with the orderly officer, retired to his own.

Silence and darkness fell upon the Spanish Farm, only broken by the steps of the sentries, the change of guard, and the dull mutter and star-shell flicker from the line, and for some hours all those human beings that lay in and around the old house, lost consciousness of their hopes, fears, and wants.

*   *   *   *

English officers and men who billeted in the Spanish Farm (and practically the whole English Army must have passed through or near it at one time or another) to this day speak of it as one of the few places they can still distinguish in the blur of receding memories, one of the few spots of which they have nothing but good to tell. In part this may be easily explained. The old house was comparatively roomy, well kept, water-tight. There was less overcrowding, no leaking roof to drip on one's only dry shirt—and besides, though

the regulations were more strictly observed here
than anywhere, that very fact gave almost an
impression of home—order, cleanliness, respect
ruled here yet a little—but perhaps there is
another reason—perhaps houses, so old and so
continually handled by human beings, have almost
a personality of their own : perhaps the Spanish
Farm that had sheltered Neapolitan mercenaries
fighting the French, Spanish Colonists fighting
the Flemish, French fighting English or Dutch—
and now English and Colonials fighting Germans
—perhaps the old building bent and brooded
over these last of its many occupants—perhaps
knew a little better than other houses what men
expected of it.

*　　　*　　　*　　　*

Madeleine thought no more of the War, and
the population it had brought to the Spanish
Farm, until half-past seven, when the mess orderlies began to prepare breakfast. Obstinately
refusing to allow anyone to touch her stove, she
cooked that incomprehensible meal of oat-soup
("porridge" they called it !), and bacon and
eggs, after which she knew, they ate orange confiture. She, her father, and the farm hands,
had long taken their lump of bread and bowl of
coffee, standing. Her attention was divided
between the hum of the separator in the dairy and
her washing drying on the line, when she heard
her father's voice calling: "Madeleine, leinsche !"

LA PATRIE EST EN DANGER

("Little Madeleine!"). She called out that she was in the kitchen.

The old man came, moving more quickly than usual, voluble in Flemish, excited. The soldiers had moved out all the flax-straw lying in the long wooden drying-shed behind the house, on the pasture, and all the machines, reapers and binders, drills and rakes. Moreover, they had taken for firewood hop-poles that had been expressly forbidden.

Madeleine washed her hands at the sink, saying she would see about it. But she was saved the trouble. Her father went out into the yard, unable to keep still in his impatience, and she heard him in altercation with old Adams. They drifted into the mess-room. As she was drying her hands, there was a knock on the kitchen door, and she saw her father ushering in the dark young officer of the evening before. Her brow cleared. She had not the least doubt she could " manage " the young man.

The young man surpassed expectations. Madeleine found it unnecessary to keep to her rather limited English. His French, while not correct, was expansive. He admitted her version of the farmer's rights under Billeting Law, but would not accept the sum, running into hundreds of francs, which Jerome Vanderlynden, typical peasant at a bargain, asked for compensation. It appeared that the quiet-looking young man knew something of flax culture and more of agricultural machinery. He quoted within a very little the cost of re-stacking the flax, oiling the machinery, with the price of two burnt hop-poles. He offered forty francs.

Old Vanderlynden made his usual counter : " What if I go to Brigade Head-quarters about it ! "

" Then you will get nothing at all. They are too busy, and we move on to-day ! "

The old man laughed and slapped his leg.

Madeleine, knowing by experience that the officer had been authorized to spend fifty francs (a sum which appealed to the English, being recognizable as a couple of sovereigns), began to respect him, took the money, and signed the receipt.

Left alone, old Jerome remarked that the young man was very well brought up. Madeleine was looking carefully through her pots and pans to see that nothing had disappeared into the big mess-box.

From the window she saw the battalion paraded, and watched them move off, as she passed hastily from room to room, counting things. Her father was round the outbuildings. The last to go was old Adams with the wagons. A great stillness fell on the old farm, the litter of papers, tins and ashes, and all the unmistakable atmosphere of a crowded place suddenly deserted.

*　　*　　*　　*

16

LA PATRIE EST EN DANGER

The day following the departure of the battalion was fine and still. Even the Front was quieting down. After the early midday meal of soup and bread, Madeleine put on her second-best frock, washed, did her hair, spent a little time over her hands, and putting on her fur but no hat, picked her way over the cobbles, and left the farm by the main gate.

She walked with the ease of a person of perfect health, who knew what she wanted and where she was going, and who had habitually no time to stroll, no need to think. The clumsiness of a life of hard physical labour had been corrected by a good education, and she might well have passed, in her dress that had so evidently been best, and was going to be everyday, for an English girl. Only the boots and the hatless head marked her for a follower of the continental tradition, though her strong ankles and round neck would have well supported the low shoes and simple felt or straw of an outdoor Englishwoman.

She said nothing to her father or to the farm-hands as to her errand. No one inquired. For a long while, ever since she had left the convent school, she had been mistress of her own actions and of other people's. Old Vanderlynden, if he ever spoke of her to others, used not the peasant's usual " Ma fille "—" my little girl," but " Ma demoiselle "—" my young lady." Her dress indicated nothing, for etiquette forbade her

going beyond the farm in her old worn " everyday " and apron, clogs and upturned sleeves.
Old men and women and children were ploughing, manuring and weed-burning in the fields
bordering the hedgeless road. She spoke to no
one, and no one spoke to her. She met them all
once a week, at Mass, and that was sufficient.
One or two of them, glancing at her straight figure
and level, unswerving gait, glanced at each other
and grinned. The usual surmises were probably
made, for it was known that she was keeping
company with none of the young men of her
generation before they were all hurried off to the
War—and it was plainly unnatural that a good-
looking young woman with a dowry should not
be sought in marriage. These surmises were all
the more interesting because nothing definite
was known.

Some hundreds of yards before reaching the
Lille-Calais road, Madeleine passed under the
shadow of one of those little woods of oak, crowning a small conical hill, that constitute the only
untilled plots of the hard-worked Flemish border.
Like its counterpart in all the neighbouring par-
ishes, this wood also was called the " Kruysabel "
or Poplar-cross, on account of the crucifix that
hid in its highest and thickest part, where its five
" rides " met in a tiny clearing. To the south of
this clearing was a little hunting shelter, brick,
with mock-Gothic windows and leaded lights,
encircled by a timber-pillared verandah, on which

the thatch of the eaves descended, in the worst
style of Lille garden-furnishing (" rustic work " in
England). After entering the wood by a wicket,
it was to this erection that Madeleine mounted by
a soft squashy " ride " between impenetrable walls
of oak sapling, planted as close as it would grow,
and cut regularly, section by section, according to
age, so that little could be seen but slim straight
grey-green stems on all sides.

Arrived at the little clearing on the summit, the
girl took out a key and entered the hunting shelter.
The ornamental porch led straight into a dining-
place almost filled by the long table surrounded
by benches. The porch and windows filled the
north wall, a great open brick-hearth with fire-
dogs, the western. Opposite was a long rack of
antlers, false or real, for greatcoats, guns and
bags. On the remaining side was a partition
pierced by two doors. The apartment was clean
and well kept—nor was this wonderful to anyone
who could have seen Madeleine produce feather
brush and duster, and go carefully along the
pine-boarded wainscot, round mouldings and
window-ledges, and along the frames of the photographs of many a jolly party—photographs in
which a man, appearing variously from middle
age to past it, moustached and whiskered in the
fashion of his youth—which must have been the
fall of the Second Empire—and a youth who
passed to manhood in the newest group—were
surrounded by male companions who tended to

be less and less hairy the newer the picture—and women in every fashion from crinolines to gaiters and deerstalkers—live horses and dogs and dead birds and beasts, on a background of hunting shelter and trees. Madeleine hardly paused to gaze at one, but passed on, chasing spiders, fly-marks, dust, and looking for damp or wormholes. She was far from being a person to stand in front of a photograph while there was work to do.

Next she opened the left-hand door and peered into the little kitchen almost filled by the vase-and-coffin-style stove, at which she and others had cooked many a hot-pot and lapin-chasseur. All was in order here, and she only glanced to see that no invading hand had touched the stacked fuel, and that the iron-ringed flagstone that opened on a diminutive cellar had not been moved. She left the kitchen. Before the other door some little animation gleamed through the naturally passive, almost defensive expression—behind which she habitually concealed her thoughts. Entering this third apartment, a little upholstered lounge, twelve feet square, she closed the door softly and stood a moment without moving. It had been originally a gun-room, but the present Baron, her father's proprietor, owner of two thousand hectares of shooting of which this shelter was the centre, had turned it into a withdrawing-room for ladies, as their presence at the shooting parties became more and more usual. A divan ran under the curtained windows, west and south, a tiny fireplace was beside the door, while a corner had been carved off the kitchen for toilet purposes. Otherwise it was pine boarded and upholstered in plaited straw like the rest of the building. But the straw-surfaces were covered with cushions, mats and covers, chiefly Oriental, and all collected, like the Flemish china on the walls, and the fancy photographs, "Kruysabel by Moonlight," "Morning in the Woods," etc., etc., by Georges, the present Baron's son.

*   *   *   *

It was this very Georges—spoiled, lovable, perverse, self-indulgent, whose taste and personality penetrated and overcame the rococo-rustic architecture and upholstery—that Madeleine had met in this very room, every time she could and he would, all that summer that led up to the declaration of war. How many times they had spent the catholic five to seven o'clock—she protected by endless subterfuges and evasions—he coming easily of right—she was far from counting. Nor did she cast back in her mind to the commencement of the thing. Indeed, there had been nothing remarkable about it. It happened like this :

Her father was the old Baron's chief tenant and head gamekeeper (as that office is understood in France). She had known Georges as a thin, dark-eyed, imperious, tyrannical boy. As a girl she had helped carry the materials of the midday feast, that, cooked and served at the Kruysabel, was the converging-point of the morning drives of the Baron's shooting parties. The last shoot of the spring of 1914 had finished in darkness, and she had been left, as usual, to clear up. Her basket packed, the place all squared-up and tidy, she had stood by candle-light, munching a strip of buttered spiced-bread and finishing, careless of the dregs, the last of a bottle of Burgundy that her Flemish soul loved as only a Flemish soul can. She had caught Georges' prominent brown eyes on her, more than once during the day, as she moved about, waiting at table. Conscious of looking her best, this had pleased her, beneath her preoccupation with her duties of cooking and serving. Moreover, she had a good day's work behind her (the Baron paid well if he was satisfied), and the Burgundy warmed her heart.

She heard footsteps behind her, and a tune hummed, and knew instinctively who it was. She kept quite still. Instinct told her that this was the most effective thing to do. Two arms, under hers, bent her backwards, and Georges fastened his lips to hers. Self-controlled, she neither called out nor resisted. Careful, even grudging in everything, when she gave, she gave generously, no half measures. That was how it had started. The most natural thing in the world. It had gone on in spasms of passion, and interludes, as far as she was concerned, of cool efficient concealment. Georges was a little younger, far

22

less healthy in mind or body, probably less strong, physically, than she. There may have been an undercurrent of almost maternal feeling on her part, and certainly not the least illusion as to the consequences of being found out. And no one had found out.

*   *   *   *

But now, as she stood in the empty room, on this October afternoon of 1915, she was as far from ruminating on the beginnings of the affair as she was from the neo-classic tower of Merville Church, visible fifteen kilometres away, in the pale sunshine, through a gap in the branches. She had to stop for a moment to get used to the atmosphere, as a diver adjusts himself to the pressure of a lower level, but it was an unconscious pause; then, pressing her lips together, she dusted and swept, opened the windows, banged mats and covers. Not that she hoped by the elaborate preparation of a room unused these fifteen months, and destined to be empty many another, to charm back the man through whom alone that room interested her. Madeleine's point of view was much simpler. Her father had charge of the shooting. She had automatically undertaken the care of the shelter. Having done so, unasked and unpaid, as part of the general unwritten arrangement between her father and the Baron, she could be trusted to go through with it, whatever happened.

Her task finished, she straightened her back and stood, hands on her hips, looking at nothing. From somewhere beyond Estaires, Givenchy or Festubert perhaps, came the sound of guns; some petty incident of the four-hundred-mile year-long battle was dragging out its squalid tragedy. Her lips moved, formed the words " Bêtes—sales bêtes ! " which mean so much more than " dirty beasts " and something more immediate than " foul brutes " in English. No sound came. All that feeling of hers was too deep down to struggle into active expression through her habitual reserve and acquiescence with current manners. Not hers to criticize or revolt, hers only to feel, to feel with all the depth of a narrow, obstinate nature. Anyone might have supposed that she was thinking of the Germans who had killed one brother, and held another prisoner since Charleroi. Could she have been induced to express herself, she might have said, from mere habit of convention, that she meant the Germans. But it was deeper than that, so deep as to be almost impersonal.

Years before, when she was but a little girl, she had stood by the bedside of her mother, dying for want of proper medical attention, the fees for which had been grudged until it was too late. Her mother had said : " Pray to the Virgin, now that you are alone ! " She had answered, sobbing : " I will pray, and I will take care of father and brothers, and they of me ! " " Pray to the

Virgin ! " the mother repeated. " She is the only one that will take care of you ! " That unique effort of expression of a life worn down with toil, and given up to save expense, had sunk into Madeleine's mind, been confirmed by the teaching of the convent school, where the nuns seemed to be perpetually clearing up the mess men made of things. When the war came Madeleine dumbly recognized it for a thing that men did. She had none of the definite sex-antagonism of an English suffragist, was affectionately tolerant of her father and brothers, and constructively tender to Georges, would have loved to have surrounded him with perpetual comfort and indulgence. But in the bulk, men were always doing things like this war. Her smouldering, almost sulky resentment had not decreased one particle during the fifteen months that had passed. For her, the day of mobilization had been catastrophic. Georges, grandson of an ennobled "industrialist" and of bourgeois blood of the official classes, surprised everybody, surprised Madeleine, surprised perhaps himself. The manifesto " La Patrie est en danger " had just been issued. He seemed to have swallowed its sentiments whole. His papers arrived, and found him in uniform—he was (of course) in the cuirassiers. He mounted and rode off. Like so many others, the indolent expensive young man lost all thought of anything except what he deemed " duty."

THE SPANISH FARM

Madeleine, who knew as well as anyone that his depot would be at Lille, had taken her stand, that August morning, just inside the gate of the Kruysabel. She had chosen that place for easy concealment, and she knew he must pass that way ; she was prepared to give him anything he might want. He passed her at the trot, looking rather fine in his regimentals, and well mounted. He raised his hand to the salute, but did not draw rein. She had gone home and taken up her work where she had laid it down.

Going about the endless jobs of a farmer's daughter, her slow-moving temper had risen and risen. She knew Georges, his impulses, his absorption in the matter that held him for the moment, his spoiled thriftlessness. He would rush into military life, engulf himself in it, never thinking for a moment to take his fill of happiness first. He would not write. She hoped he would not. There would be no means of keeping the arrival of his letters secret from the whole village. Nor would she write to him. She made no bones over social distinctions, upheld them rather. He was the young master. It was not for her to write. This left a great ache in her, for which she presently found a partial cure. It came to her as she was packing up parcels of small luxuries for her brothers. She packed a third one, more carefully than the first two. As the billeting of English troops on the farm became increasingly regular, she managed to vary and improve that third parcel, obtaining from the—to her—sumptuously overstocked canteens and private presents of the men in khaki—tinned stuff, toilet wares, and the beautiful English cigarettes Georges loved. She posted this third packet from Hazebrouck each weekly market day, for however well known she was to the farming community, she was a stranger to the small postal and other officials of the railway town. She comforted herself that if anything (it was always called " anything " by the women of the War, whatever their nationality) had happened to Georges the parcel would be returned. She was far from picturing the trenches to herself. So, with steady, profitable work at the farm, now a camp and barrack as well, with a weekly parcel to send, and a weekly visit to the shelter at Kruysabel, the interminable months had passed. People—her father with one son dead and one a prisoner—her sister, down in Laventie, within bullet-range of the trenches—got accustomed to the war.

But not Madeleine.

*   *   *   *

So, as she stood in the fading light of the October sunset, resting a moment before she returned to the farm, there was nothing petty or personal in the grim set of her features, the slow-burning anger of her eyes. She might have posed there for a symbolic figure of Woman contemplating Fate. She stood straight in her neat, almost careful dress, bought with one eye on looks and one on usefulness, solid well-kept boots and stockings, thick but without hole or wrinkle. Large boned, but so close-knit that she did not look disproportionately broad, her figure, kept in check by hard work and frugal feeding, promised to grow thick only with middle age. Anyone looking at her face would have said, " What a handsome woman," not " What a pretty girl." There was something below the surface that kept the red lips closed in their firm line, the round chin lifted, the grey eyes and level brows serene. Her dark hair, which she kept, while at work, tied in a duster, was neat and smooth. Her skin had the pallor of health.

That internal quality that made her simple shapeliness so much more arresting than any trick of dimple, glance, or elaborate preparation and high colour, was, like anything else worth having, the gradual distillation of the hard-lived generations gone before. How much of it came from the cultivators who had hung on to that low ridge between the marshes and the sea, as French and Norman, English, Burgundian and Spaniard swept over it, and how much from the Spanish blood of Alva's colonists who had held the old block-house-farm amid all the unfriendliness of climate, native inhabitants, and chance, none can now say.

Jerome Vanderlynden had a hook nose and beady brown eyes. Madeleine rather took after

28

her mother, a Delplace of Bailleul, in her straight nose and fair complexion. But there it was, outwardly, obstinacy ; inwardly—something more. It was that "something more" that clouded her smooth forehead and flashed in her stabbing, side-to-side stare. She never even dreamed of envying the properly married women who had received official and private recognition of the trouble the War had brought them. Nor did she stop to pity the hundreds of thousands of women of irregular position, who had been abandoned on the outbreak of hostilities, without resources. Her feeling, if almost impersonal, was simple, direct. This War, this "Bêtise," this great Stupidity had taken Georges from her. She would be even with it. She put away her duster and brush, wrapped herself in her fur, and locking up, descended the ride to the wicket without glancing at the scuttling rabbits, crossed two arable fields, by their narrow grass borders, and so through the north pasture entered the house by the plank bridge and the scullery door. Hanging her fur in her room, she slipped on her long blue apron, went to the kitchen, and began doing the next thing.

* * * *

Nearly a week passed before the advance-party of a new battalion, consisting of an interpreter in the blue uniform of the French Mission and an English officer, rode into the courtyard. They were received by Madeleine, who gave them coffee and began to explain herself in English as usual, as to what she was disposed to do, and charge, and the rules she expected to be observed. The Englishman was the usual square, blond, sheepishly-grinning grown-up boy, who nodded and said " All right " whenever there was a pause. The interpreter was a middle-aged commercial traveller for a colonial house, who talked glibly and respectfully, while under the table his foot pursued Madeleine's. The arrangements completed, Madeleine left the two, who had obviously lunched well in Hazebrouck or Cassel, to measure up and ticket the various rooms, barns, and stables, according to their requirements.

It was again her day for the Kruysabel, and she went to her room, slipping off her apron and her stained and mended dress, to tidy herself. Her room was a small cell-like apartment looking out across the moat to the north pasture. The distempered walls were marked with damp, but the tiled floor was clean and the places round the window where the plaster had come away were hidden by short curtains. Before this window, which was in a corner, stood a chest of drawers, bearing the cheap deal looking-glass and an old inlaid box containing the girl's few treasures. The remaining wallspace of the outside wall was filled by the great wooden bedstead, above the head of which was a little china bracket carrying the inevitable sprig of box-tree. The bed came so far down the little room that there was only place for a wooden chair between its foot and the door, on the other side of which stood a tall press, reaching to the ceiling, and a wooden washstand, surmounted by a shelf that held the relics of Madeleine's first communion under a glass bell, such as used to be seen in England encasing Dresden clocks. The washstand just allowed for the drawers to open.

Thus, as she did her hair before the glass in the window, Madeleine could see her door softly opened, to admit the interpreter, who had drawn off his boots and tiptoed in, his brown eyes gleaming greasily at the sight of her bare arms and neck, muttering : " What luck ! " The words died on shaking lips and the creased eyelids fluttered over downcast eyes, as she turned in cold fury : " Get out of my bedroom ! "

He hesitated, and catching the ewer of common white china she slung it forward with the force of muscles accustomed to tossing swedes to feed the mashing-machine. It broke on his forehead, cutting his eyebrow and deluging him with water. With a gasp he was gone.

She called to Berthe to bring a swab and broom. When the mess was cleared : " That imbecile of an interpreter ! " she said.

" It is a dirty type," grunted the philosophic Berthe. Madeleine forgot the incident.

She recalled it, however, before the new battalion had been under the roof of the Spanish

31

Farm many hours. They broke every rule, stole, destroyed, trespassed, and worst of all, left open the gate from the pasture to the " plain " (the level range of arable), so that the cattle got out and had to be chased back. Madeleine, having expostulated with N.C.O.'s and men, finally appealed to the Major, who sent for the Adjutant. The latter, not allowing for Madeleine's English, said bluntly that the interpreter had informed him that the people were Germans in disguise, and would be the better for a lesson.

Madeleine interposed with such energy and point that the officers promised, in order to get rid of her, to issue orders. Not believing in stones left unturned, Madeleine also wrote to the Chief of the French Mission at Cassel. Then an idea struck her. She looked in her account book, where under the heading " Easthamptonshire Regiment " she had noted the name of the dark young officer who spoke French so well, Lieutenant Geoffrey Skene. She wrote to him as well, asking if he would come over and intercede with the troops.

*　　*　　*　　*

The day after, the battalion left, the Major giving her twenty francs for wood burnt, fowls and eggs. As there had been over twenty officers in the mess and nearly nine hundred men in the battalion, Madeleine added up the billeting and mess money and was content. She received an

acknowledgment of her letter from the French
Mission, but nothing else. Again peace and
emptiness fell on the Spanish Farm.

Again, nearly a week elapsed, when Madeleine,
stirring the midday soup, saw an officer ride into
the courtyard. She called to her father, who
was sorting haricots. He went out and returned
with Lieutenant Skene.

Madeleine did not understand the English and
it did not worry her. She had indeed required
this young man to deal with a difficulty, but the
need had passed. Still, he might be useful, and
she invited him to stay to lunch, calling to Berthe
to kill a fowl, while her father got up a bottle of
Burgundy. She heard politely a long explanation as to the receipt of her letter, and the im-
possibility of replying sooner, owing to conditions
prevailing in the trenches. She understood what
was said, but paid little heed, not being interested.
She had found this young man so far " well
brought up " and " malin," " sharp at money "
in contest with her father. She now began to
see that he was " serviable," " willing." This
thought, striking against her eternal preoccupation with Georges, kindled a spark.

It was when the young officer mentioned that
he lay in the trenches next some French troops
that the spark caught, flamed, became an idea.
She showed nothing, of course, presiding with
her usual competence at the long Flemish midday meal, which she felt to be his due, after having

got him to come so far on his useless errand.
But as the four courses followed one another, and a
carafe of beer gave place to more Burgundy, she
was thinking. Her father went back to work,
leaving the Lieutenant smoking over his coffee
and glass of Lille gin.

She began to question him with infinite caution,
trying to find out what his strange view of life
might be. She made up her mind, after rallying
him (as was rather the fashion) on his conquests
of her sex in France, that he was very innocent,
well brought up, sharp at money, willing, and
now she added in her mind, "rather a child,"
"un peu enfant." It did not displease her.
On the contrary, it was all to the good. She
rather expected the English to be like that. He
did not take the subject up and feign interest in
her, as a Frenchman would have done, but remained serious. She was therefore obliged to
say right out what was in her mind. It was to
ask him, next time he went up to the trenches,
next to the French troops, to try and obtain news
of Georges for her. She had heard that his regiment was in the northern sector. She formed
no idea of the trenches, of the camps and resting-
places next to them. She simply said what she
wanted. Once the words were out she had to
use all her self-control. The sound of her re-
quest, the speaking aloud of what had been going
round and round in her mind for so long, brought
a rush of feeling such as she had not experienced

34

since the first day of mobilization. She bit her lips to keep back tears and sobs. Then she was glad to hear the Lieutenant promising to do what he could. There was some difficulty about it, apparently, she was not curious to understand. She was glad she had asked the Englishman, realizing now how the thing sounded, and what a tale a Frenchman would have made of it. All she cared about now was for this young man to go—she was aching with the effort of restraint— and get her the news she wanted. She had no clear idea what. She pictured in a dim way Georges sending a message that he was all right, and making an appointment to meet her, in St. Omer—Calais—where he liked. Further than that her imagination could not take her.

She thanked the young man cordially, and offered him more gin. He refused, and went away, assuring her that he was at her service in this as in other matters. She forgot him before he was out of the yard, and fearing that she would cry—a thing she had not done since she was a tiny girl—she went to her room. But she did not cry. She sat on the wooden chair at the foot of the bed, her hands on the wooden rail, her face upon her hands. Nothing happened. She soon went back to her work, for her feelings were even worse in that little room of hers than in the big kitchen where she had so much to do. Gradually her heart ceased to thump, her eyes to smart. But she had taken the first active step towards getting

Georges back——towards that recovery of anything taken from her, that was her deepest instinct. And she knew that she would not stop at any first step——not she !

*　　*　　*　　*

It took more than a mere European war twenty miles off to interrupt the regular life of the Spanish Farm. Troops came and troops went, and Madeleine watched them, watched the payments made by the messes for extra accommodation and cooking, and the weekly payments through the Mairie for billeting and stabling, watched the storing of the crops, the thrashing, the milking, the feeding of the fowls. Every week she went to market, sold what she could, bought as little as possible, and sent her parcel, surreptitiously, from the post office. She neither heard nor saw anything of Georges. She neither heard nor saw anything of Lieutenant Skene. But, sure enough, on the first opportunity, she was obliged to try to get news of Georges.

It happened, as winter came on, that " the château " had need of some things, eggs, and hare pâté——nowhere so good as at the Spanish Farm——and Madame la Baronne wanted some sewing done, rather special, better than any of her women could do. A message came via the Baron, who shouted from horseback, as he rode by, to Vanderlynden, at work in the plain. Old Vanderlynden handed it on to Madeleine, as he bent in an attitude half of prayer, half a crouching ape's, over the midday soup.

Madeleine nodded and told him to put in the horse—not that she could not have done it, but she must clean herself. Accordingly, half an hour later, there might have been seen issuing from the yard of the Spanish Farm, over the brick bridge, along the earth road that divided the manor pasture, out by the brick-pillared gate on to the road, surely the oldest, most repaired of high black gigs, drawn by an old white horse whose sonorous walk took it along at perhaps two miles an hour. Framed in the dark aperture of the hood, upright, expressionless, sat Madeleine, bareheaded, but in her best dress, holding the reins in a gloved hand, basket between her feet. Silent, expressionless, she may have been, but when she turned into the Lille-Calais road and met a string of English transport, limbers and wagons, it was noticeable that the Quartermaster-Sergeant, after glancing at her face, instead of shouting to her to get out of the way, turned in his saddle and shouted to the drivers, " Right o' the road ! "

She came to the village and crossed the empty Grand' Place, where the old houses stared unchanged over the notice-boards of the offices of the Head-quarters of an English Division, and the church, newly faced with red brick, showed the zeal of the pious Flemings. Turning sharply out of this, she mounted, at the snail pace of the old white horse, a steep street between little houses of people who had retired to live on about the equivalent of forty pounds English per annum (as people do in France). It ended in a great eighteenth-century iron grille, the entry to the château. The central gates stood open and she drove straight along a road deep between high banks covered with shrubs, which followed for some fifty yards the old line of the moat, until she came under the back part of the château where a broad terrace of gravel separated the basement offices from the kitchen garden. Leaving the old horse, with perfect confidence, looking down his nose into a laurel bush, Madeleine took her basket on her arm, and entered the great square kitchen.

One of the things that renders life so easy in France is the absence of change. Anywhere outside Paris, and often in it, change seems to have worn itself out, and to have ceased. In that remote corner of Flanders, Madeleine had no shyness, hesitation, or doubt, in entering the house of her father's landlord and her lover's mother. She would not have dreamed of entering by the front. No less would she have thought of leaving the house without seeing Madame la Baronne in person. She was not alone in this. The establishment was ruled by a lean, gaunt, grey-moustached person, discernible to be of the female sex only by her clothes, named Placide. Just as for Madeleine, so for Placide, life was an easy riddle. She knew her place to a hair's breadth, between God, and her master and her mistress, on the one hand, and the servants, tenants, tradespeople on the other. The great square block of a house, the main building of the older castle, whose wings had been thrown into its moat, whose forecourt had become flower gardens in the revolution of 1790, went on its even way under her iron rule, undisturbed by wars. The presence of a mess of English officers in the Baron's quarters, east of the main staircase, the absence of young Master Georges, of all the men-servants, and of some of the women who had gone to work on farms, did not throw Placide out of her stride. When Madeleine entered, she was standing with her back to the dresser with its shining pots and pans, telling a maid-servant her duties. The following conversation ensued :

" Good morning, Madeleine, how goes it ? "
" Good morning, Placide, not too badly ! "
" You have brought the things ! "
" Here they are."
" What will you have to take ? "
" Nothing, thank you ! "
" Come, a glass of beer, a cup of coffee ! "
" Nothing, thank you all the same ! "
" But you will say ' Good day ' to Madame ! "
" Why yes, if Madame wishes it."

This little formality, for both speakers had said just those words hundreds of times and knew them by heart, being over, Placide went to see if Madame were free to see Madeleine, and Madeleine sipped coffee as though she had not refused it, and gossiped with the girls.

She was then ushered through the paved and plastered back passage, smelling of all the game that had been carried through it, and of all the corks that had been drawn in it, to the front hall floored with black and white stone, on which stood heavy old furniture, a little of each period and a good deal of 1860 to 1870, between walls that were painted in landscape as a background to the plaster statues of classical deities and symbolic figures of the virtues, holding lamps. From this, the high double doors opened into the drawing-room or salon, where Madame sat since the use of Monsieur's apartments by English troops had forced her to relinquish her boudoir to serve as his bedroom.

Madame la Baronne d'Archeville had been married when the Empress Eugénie was the first lady of Europe, and taking marriage very seriously, had never tried to change since. Although she had neither the height nor carriage of her imperial example, she continued in 1915 doing her hair and wearing her clothes as she had begun, and the effect was all her own. Herself of high bourgeois blood, she had married when told to, without demur, the Baron, who, son of an army contractor and, so he said, great-grandson of an emigré of 1792, had re-purchased with money made out of républiques and empires, what those empires and républiques had taken from his ancestors, real or imaginary.

The room in which Madame sat looked like it. Originally the banqueting hall of the small feudal castle from which the château had grown, it ran from back to front of the modernized building, with two tall windows looking on to the kitchen garden behind, and two others, opposite, looking on to the flower garden in front, and over trees and village roofs into the rich undulations of the plain. The great beams that held the roof were visible, but below them the walls that had been panelled were papered cream and gold. Against this background hung two rows of pictures, the upper row smallish and very dark, displaying, as far as could be seen, grim old men in more or less armour, and stolid ladies in stuffs, laces and jewels hardly less resisting. The lower row was composed of portraits of whiskered men in uniforms of recent eras, and women, all in evening dresses of the nineteenth century, varied by landscapes, some good, some too good to be true, in pairs. Below the pictures were marble slabs on gilt brackets, tables shining with brass inlay. The floor space was occupied with curly armed, heavily stuffed chairs and settees. It was a room into which the Second Empire seemed to have burst in flood, washing up the drift of earlier ages, and to have ebbed, leaving a carpet shiny from use.

But to Madame la Baronne, and Madeleine, no such thoughts occurred. To Madame it was her salon. To Madeleine it was Madame's salon. To Madeleine, Madame said :

" Good day, Madeleine. All goes well at the farm ? "

" Yes, Madame la Baronne. I hope that the health of Monsieur and Madame is good, and that there is good news of Monsieur Georges."

She stood, square planted and upright, not quite so near the door as a servant, not quite so near Madame's chair as a visitor. She was perfectly conscious that on her left, in the curve of the grand piano, was a red, blue and white draped easel on which was a picture in oils of Georges, as a boy, in a white sailor suit, lips parted, eyes staring a little, evidently just going to say, " I want so-and-so," in his spoiled way. But she spoke his name without tremor, and heard the reply :

" Thank you, we are well; we have no news of my son, but that is good news, is it not ? "

" Yes, Madame. I have brought the things."

" Very well. Placide will pay you. Good day."

" Good day, Madame la Baronne, and thank you."

Backing with a curtsy to the door, she let herself out, took her money from Placide, received her basket with her cloths and terrine, jerked up the head of the old white horse, and drove back

42

to the farm. She had got what she wanted—the assurance of no ill news of Georges.

*   *   *   *

That evening, in the lamp-lit salon, after Madame had said, " There is nothing more ; good night, Placide," there was silence only broken by the Baron puffing his cigar. He supported the war very badly. He was too old to serve and was prevented from fishing or shooting by English water-supply officers, who dammed up and filtered his waters, and by French Gendarmerie Commandants, who stopped his supplies of cartridges. At last he exploded :

" Nothing ever happens in this cursed war. You, what have you done to-day ? "

Madame la Baronne replied, after a moment's silence that was partly protest at his manners and partly some tiny instinctive defensiveness, " I have seen Madeleine Vanderlynden ! "

" Ah, she brought the ham and the hare pâté ! "

" Yes." Madame was struggling with that tiny instinct—could not quite catch what it prompted—her feeling only materialized into the words :

" She has bold eyes ! "

" It is a fine girl. Probably she knows it ! " qualified the Baron, and mused.

Madame mused too. But the necessity, forced upon her early in married life with the Baron, of

43

shutting one's eyes and ears to what men did and said about women, prevented her connecting Madeleine's composure with her own family. She could only fall back on her stock complaint.

" She will never be like her mother, that poor Sylvie ! "

But irritation had supervened with the Baron : " You're not obliged to receive the girl ! "

" One has to do what one can for one's people. They wouldn't like it if one didn't say a word to them when they come with things."

" Do what you like so long as I have hare pâté," yawned the Baron. " Ugh, this war, I do nothing but yawn and sleep ! "

" I pray ! " said Madame to herself, and rose to go to the little " chapel " in the turn of the stairs to do so.

*   *   *   *

Madeleine had no theory of the Irony of Fate. She had a merely hard experience of it, gained from watching crops and prices. Reassured as to Georges' safety by what she had heard at the château, she took what comfort she could.

Three days after her visit, she was sewing and mending by the kitchen stove, using the light of the dying sunset to the last glimmer. There were no English troops in the farm on that day, and outside were the sounds of her father putting up the horses, on a background of damp late-autumn silence, and behind that, the muffled

vibration of the eternal battle, that made the
window-panes tremble ever so little.

Suddenly there came the sound of whistling—
the last bars of the well-worn tune :

> " Marguérite . . . . .
> Marguérite, donne-moi ton cœur ! "

and shouted greetings. Then her father's
slouching tread and a brisk military stride.
Then her father's voice :

" Mad'leine, here is Victor Dequidt, home on
leave ! "

She got up, pushed the ever-ready coffee-pot
over the heat of the fire, and greeted the guest.
He was the son of a neighbouring farmer, and if
she ever bothered her head about such things,
Madeleine was perhaps conscious deep down in
herself that he liked her more than a little. They
had played together as children, grown to adol-
escence together, had experiences in common,
wandering in the Kruysabel. But ever since her
mother's death had forced her to early maturity,
Madeleine had been very busy, then, with
Georges, very busy and very happy, and since
the War, very busy and preoccupied. Any
memories of Victor hardly disturbed the surface
of her mind. If he liked to follow her about
with his blue eyes, and pay her small compliments,
why, let him. Most men looked at her, so might
he. She poured him out coffee, and some of the
rum she had got from the quartermasters of

various English units, and listened politely, but without interest, to his talk.

It was the usual talk of men on leave. All that he said was being said in English, French, German, Italian, during years, whenever men got home for a few brief days. It was about food, railways, jokes, old acquaintances—never about the cosmic murder in which they were engaged, or their daily decreasing belief that they might escape alive. In the middle of the commonplaces that she had heard from different lips a hundred times in that kitchen, Madeleine heard the words :

" It was a good job, that stretcher-bearing business at the hospital, miles from the line— good food—a bunk to sleep in at night, and who do you think was the last stretcher-case I carried ? "

Silence. Old Vanderlynden was not good at guessing. Madeleine was bored. Victor went on :

" Why, the young Baron Georges ! "

Silence again. Old Vanderlynden, who could hardly see to fill his pipe, said :

" It's as dark as a nigger's back in here ! " and held a paper spill to the candle on the mantelshelf.

Madeleine cried with a stamp of her foot :

" Don't light up ! don't light up ! "

Her father obediently lit his pipe, knocked out the half-burnt spill against the fireplace and put it back.

Victor, disappointed at the way his anecdote was received, said gallantly :

" One sees you are a good housekeeper, and not one to burn good money ! "

But Madeleine was just succeeding, by sheer will-power in swallowing—swallowing down It —the maniacal desire that had come rushing up from her heart into her head—the strong frenzy of a strong nature—bidding her catch up the great steel harl from the hearth and smash in the heads—not so much of her father and Victor, but of these two men—prototypes of all the other careless, mischievous, hopeless men, that had let Georges be hurt in their insane war. She swallowed, and the fury of that instant was gone, battened down, under control. She replied to Victor in a steady off-hand voice :

" Oh no, we have plenty of candles from the English. After all, you might as well light up, Father ! "

As he did so, the old man asked :

" What had he the matter with him, the poor young baron ? "

" He had become consumptive, owing to the life."

As the candle took heart and shone, Madeleine's courage rose to meet the necessity for showing nothing and finding out everything which she deliberately courted. Sure of herself, she said gently :

" To which base-hospital did you say he was

going ? " She saw her mistake in a moment. She was not so completely mistress of herself as she had thought. No hospital had been mentioned. But there was nothing subtle about Victor. He was only too pleased to have interested her. He replied :

" The English hospital in tents at Naes' farm, there beside the St. Omer line. Ours are full."

His gossiping talk flickered on like the candle flame—dim and alone. Madeleine and her father said scarcely a word, the former deliberately, wanting to be alone, the latter lacking the habit of speech. As no interest was shown and no further refreshment offered, Victor eventually rose to go. They bade him good night at the door, locked up, and turned to their rooms, with their usual brief word of nightly affection. The old man was snoring directly. Madeleine lay for hours on her back, her eyes burning at the dim ceiling of her little room, her legs and feet straight and rigid, hands clasped on her thumping heart. Surely he was a lucky man for whom she planned and schemed and longed so in her short, hard-earned time of rest !

*   *   *   *

The next day Jerome Vanderlynden and Madeleine set out in the dark early morning and reached Hazebrouck before most of the market had forgathered. This the old man understood and agreed to. One got one's own price by this

means from people who were in a hurry. What
he did not understand was why Madeleine had
on her very best instead of her second best that
she usually wore to market, without a hat. Incurious and incapable of challenging her decisions,
he said nothing. The stuff sold well. By eight
o'clock the basket and receptacles were almost
empty. Then Madeleine said :

" We must go and see the young baron."

" What do we want to go tra'passin' over there
for ? "

" Because Victor may be wrong. The Baron
and Madame had not heard the other day."

" That's their affair."

" If it's true, they'll be glad enough to know."

" It will cost something."

" Leave the money to me."

She had made up her mind and she was going.
Independent as were few girls of her sort, she
was too conventional to risk the journey alone.
That would be to court scandal. So her father
must come with her.

At the station they got into some difficulty
about tickets. The line was almost entirely
military. The grey-haired Commissioner was
an acquaintance.

" What are you going to do there, you
two ? "

Madeleine pushed before her father.

" We are going to see a wounded relative in
hospital ! "

49   E

"Well, you can have privilege tickets. All you want is the certificate of the Mairie."

Madeleine knew better than to argue on such a point. She drew the old man outside.

"Get down to the 'Golden Key' and come back with the cart. Look sharp!"

"Why not drive all the way?"

"Twenty kilometres there and twenty back; we should not be home all night, and supposing an English regiment comes to the farm when I'm not there?"

One of the great advantages Madeleine possessed over her father was that she could think so much quicker. The old man had fetched the cart, Madeleine had done her shopping, and they were two kilometres on the road home before he had thought of the next objection:

"What are you going to say to Blanquart?"

Blanquart was the schoolmaster and secretary of the Mairie.

"That I want a certificate that we have relatives at the war."

"But that won't get you a cheap ticket to visit the young baron in hospital?"

"You leave it to me."

Obedient, the old man left it.

Blanquart was not at the Mairie, he was measuring fields for an "expertise," a professional assessment.

Leaving the cart on the road, Madeleine lifted her best skirt and stepped over the clods to him.

He was busy and interested in his job, and didn't
want to be dragged home to the Mairie. At her
suggestion he wrote the certificate on the next
fair page of the big square pocket-book he was
covering with figures. He was not very curious
about the matter. The Vanderlyndens were the
best-known family in the parish. The loss of the
two boys was no secret. He was asked every
day for the endless certificates, questionnaires,
lists and returns by which France is governed :
" You are going to join the Society of the Friends
of the Prisoners of War, I suppose ? "

Madeleine let him suppose, only murmuring
that one did what one could in such times.

He wrote : " I, Anastasius Amadeus Blanquart, Secretary of the Mairie of the Commune
of Hondebecq, certify that Vanderlynden, Jerome, cultivator, has male relatives mobilized for
military service," and signed.

" Now you'll want the official stamp. Ask my
little Cécile. She knows where it is."

" Perfectly. And we thank you many times."

" There is nothing. Always at your service."

" Good day, Monsieur Blanquart."

Sure enough, at the schoolhouse, also in all
Flemish villages the office of the Mairie, little
Cécile Blanquart was proud to affix the official
stamp, with its " République Française, Commune de Hondebecq " inscription in violet ink.

So back went the old gig, down the same road
it had just come. In the distance rumbled the

battle. Each side of the hedgeless road with its grassy stone pavé and "dirt" paths, the rich heavy lands gleamed with moisture in their nakedness, in the pastures the last leaves of the elms fluttered down upon thick grass that soaked and soaked. Flanders, the real Flanders, the strip of black alluvial soil between the chalky downs of France and the gravelly or stony waste border where the Germanic peoples begin, was preparing herself for another fruitful year, as she had, time out of mind, in war and in peace, paying as little attention to this war as to any other of the long series she had seen. And across her breast, on that Route Nationale that a French Emperor had built with stone from Picardy, went old Vanderlynden, child of her soil, inheritor of her endless struggle, and Madeleine, the newer, more self-conscious, better-educated generation, perhaps even more typical of her country than her father, showing the endless adaptability of her mixed border race, absorbing the small steps of human progress, and emerging even more Flemish than before.

The old man, in his black suit and high-crowned, peaked Dutch cap, sat almost crouching on the seat of the gig, knees nearly as high as his chin, wrists on knees, dark eyes fixed on the road ahead, speaking from time to time to the old white horse, who paid no attention nor varied its wooden shamble. Madeleine, whose clothes were almost those of a modern girl of the towns, sat upright, hands folded in her lap, head erect, in face and figure just another of those strongly built, tranquil, slightly "managing" Madonnas of the pictures of the old Flemish painters, if ever Madonna had so grim an immobility, such a slow-burning, unquenchable spark in the grey eye.

They reached the 'Golden Key,' put up the horse and gig, and walked to the station. There was a train in ten minutes. They each took a bowl of coffee and slice of bread, not at the station buffet where the tariff was aimed at the hurried traveller, but at the little café outside, where the small ill-paid world employed at a French station gets itself served for twenty centimes a time less than other people. Then Madeleine went with her certificate, her own and her father's identity cards, and her hand full of small notes, to the booking-office.

"Two third-class privilege tickets to Schaexen Halte, and return, to see a wounded relative!"

The booking-clerk took the papers and looked at them.

"This is no good," he muttered through his decayed teeth.

Madeleine, with all the contempt of the comparatively free and wealthy farmer's daughter for the small railway official, and all the cunning of one who deals with beasts and the law, held her peace.

The booking-office clerk was in that category of age and infirmity which alone in those days

could exempt a man from mobilization. He
worked fifteen hours a day in a pigsty of an
office, whose glazed wicket made a perpetual
draught. He was easily flustered.

" You asked for two privilege tickets to go and
see a wounded relative in hospital."

" That is what I said ! "

" This certificate is incomplete ! "

Madeleine said never a word, but leaned
calmly on the ledge of the wicket, making herself
look as stupid as she could, by letting her lower
lip droop. Behind her a queue was forming.
Already there were cries of : " Come on ! "
" The train goes in five minutes," and a wag,
" They are making a film for the cinema ! "

Tears of exasperation came into the little man's
eyes and his hand began to tremble. He stamped
his foot.

" Write the name of the relative you are going
to visit."

" I have no pen."

Men were hammering on the partition and
women were saying, " Are we going to miss the
train in addition to all our other miseries ? "

The booking-office clerk flung his hairy crossed-
nibbed pen at Madeleine. She took it, and wrote
in the margin of Blanquart's certificate the name
of her dead brother, carefully using the Flemish
script, which the railway people, mainly pure
French, could not read. The paper was seized ;
the cards of identity, the privilege tickets, the

change were thrust into her hands. She moved away, counting her change and smiling a very little to herself, and giving just a glance each to the English military policeman and the French gendarme at the platform entrance, both amused spectators of the scene. Behind her, the booking-office clerk kept chewing over the words " sacred peasants," " swine's luck," and other expressions of feeling, as he jabbed the date on tickets and served them in frenzied haste to the crowd that besieged his wicket.

On the wooden benches of the third-class compartment old Vanderlynden and Madeleine found many an acquaintance. There were cries of : " How goes it, Madeleine ? " " Jerome, what are you jolly-well doing here, since when did you live St. Omer way ? "

*   *   *   *

Madeleine, who had foreseen this contingency, nudged her father, and replied for both :

" We have a little business to attend to," having made up her mind that no one would guess what it was. She was right. Thus she set running the right stream of vague gossip. For weeks after, the news ran through all the surrounding communes, and flowed back to Hondebecq, that she and her father had been to St. Omer by train. It circulated from the inn of " Lion of Flanders " to the restaurant " The Three Crownpieces," even descended to mere estaminets like the "Return from the Congo" and the "Brave Sapeur-Pompier." No one could make it out. Victor Dequidt soon rejoined his regiment, and if he mentioned the young baron, no one except Madeleine was curious enough to ask which hospital he had gone to. Nor did anyone know of Madeleine's particular interest in him. At last, when the tale got to the café-restaurant "de la Gare et de Commerce," one of the graziers or bullock merchants who used that more business quarter of the village was able to propound a theory. There was an English Forage Officer at St. Omer, and he had his depôt just exactly at Naes' farm, by the new sidings the English had had to make at Schaexen Halte for their hospital, so as to be out of the way of the bombing. No doubt old Vanderlynden had worked the trick all right with that officer (who was buying large quantities), and done well out of it. The certificate of having mobilized relatives that Blanquart had given in such a hurry (and which, of course, was known through Cécile and the other school-children), might be on account of Marcel Vanderlynden, or might be merely a blind. The original paper on which Madeleine had written her brother's name remained in the archives of the station until all were burnt in the bombardment of December, 1917.

*　　*　　*　　*

Descending at Schaexen Halte, Madeleine and

her father made their way to the block of white marquees and tents that almost filled the manor pasture of Naes' farm. In spite of the fresh air, the smell of anæsthetics and disinfectants hung over the duck-board paths and cindered drives, and mingled with the odour of cooking maconochie and the smoke of a giant incinerator that, never quenched, burned the daily load of discarded clothing and bandages, filthy with human refuse and trench mud. Near by, in the corner where Naes used to grow his maize, was a small neat cemetery of little mounds with inscribed wooden crosses, destined to grow with the years into a bigger area than the hospital and the sidings together, until lawyers had to argue out the compensation due to Naes for the expropriation. At this point luck deserted Madeleine, for no sooner had she and her father got into conversation with an orderly, than up rolled a convoy of a dozen ambulances, out ran all the available orderlies, and the whole place hummed like a railway station. There was no getting an answer to a question, and the pair were obliged to step into the nearest tent to avoid being run over. They found themselves, in the peculiar half light of such places, before a wooden table at which a sergeant was writing hurriedly. At Madeleine's question he called over his shoulder :

" What about these civilians, sir, are they allowed ? "

A young doctor came in from somewhere be-

57

hind, buckling on a belt. He spoke kindly in French, but was obviously preoccupied. There had been some French casualties in the hospital, he thought, but it had not been his tour of duty, and they had been passed on at once.

" Besides," he added, " all next-of-kin are informed if it is a serious case, and you will soon hear for certain."

Aware of the truth of this, and of her false position, Madeleine did not press the matter. She knew the English were queer about such things. So were the French, but she understood their sort of queerness and sympathized with it, not the English sort.

The officer and sergeant went outside, and began examining, questioning, listing, sorting the long line of stretchers, each with its pale, patient face above dirty blankets, a line that grew faster than it could be dealt with. Madeleine drew her father outside and sent him off to the halte on the railway, to drink a glass of beer. She herself pried about among tent-pegs and ropes, canvas flaps and damp twilight. She managed to get into one big tent with iron beds in rows, and was going from one to the other when she was stopped by a girl of her own age, in the ugly grey and red uniform and beautiful white coif of English nurses. The girl said :

" Défendu ! " She spoke with a queer accent. Madeleine had a flash of inspiration :

" I am looking for my fiancé, a French

soldier," she said in English. The girl's eyes melted.

"I'm so sorry, there are no French here, all gone!" She called an orderly to "show the lady out!"

Madeleine tried to question him, but all she got was : "Straight down the cinder track you'll find the road!" and "Now then, mum, get on, 'ow the 'ell am I to evacuate these bloody blessays with you in the gangway. 'Tisn't decent, besides!"

She made a détour and tried once more, but only once. She pushed her way into a tent behind some screens, and peeping over, saw a sergeant-major, followed by bearers with a stretcher covered by a Union Jack. They put it on the iron table, lifted the flag and began fetching water, unbinding and washing the helpless thing. She slipped away behind the screens unnoticed. She tried no more. She did not connect the dead body with Georges. She could not imagine him dead. But it was unlucky. Deep down some superstition was touched.

*   *   *   *

She rejoined her father, and they caught a train that got back to Hazebrouck at four. Suddenly she wished to be alone, felt a necessity for a moment to gather herself for the next stroke, as it were. Her father had not said a word since the hospital, but she wanted him to go away.

59

She sat in the salle d'attente and sent him for
the horse and gig. She stared in front of her at
the gathering shadows, between the sand-bagged
windows. She heard the feet of the old horse,
the rattle of the gig-wheels. Then suddenly her
father appeared with Lieutenant Skene. She had
not thought of him, but she thought fast enough
now. Quickly, using the word "fiancé" for
Georges, she explained her plight. He was the
same well-brought-up, handy, decorous young
officer. In a moment he had broken into the
Railway Transport Office, pushed aside the cor-
poral, possessed himself of the telephone and was
trying to get something definite from the hospital
as to Georges' destination after leaving the place.
He came back disappointed; they could not trace
the name.

Meantime, the fighting half of her spirit had
got its breath, and cutting short his apologies, she
went rapidly on to the next thing. Could he get
her a lift in a car or lorry to the English base to
which alone, so he said, casualties passing through
English clearing-stations would go? In a moment she saw her mistake, she had asked too
much, had run across some inexplicable—to her,
unreasonable, prejudice in the young officer's
mind. She knew well enough that it was forbidden for civilians to travel in British vehicles,
but had counted hastily on his position as an
officer and her powers of persuasion. He began
to use commonplaces, to inquire how she was

getting on with the troops at the farm. Briefly, tartly, she replied she must be getting home, and rose to go. She did not bother about the look of concern on his face, but turning to say good-bye from the gig, as it got slowly in motion, she reflected that it was foolish to throw away possible friends and their help, and called to him, "Come and see us soon." He made a gesture and she accepted the fact that he was rather taken with her. He would be.

Driving home in the twilight, however, she had only one thought—rather one feeling. This war had dealt her a blow. She admitted that, on the day's doings, she was worsted. Was she going to give in ? Not she ! Silent beside her father, up the road between the silent fields, one process only was going on in her. A hardening, a storing-up of strength. Done ? She was only just beginning !

*   *   *   *

She had plenty of time for reflection as the winter wore on. Madame la Baronne did not send down to the farm for anything special enough to be made a pretext for a visit to the château. Moreover, though she longed to go and ask boldly what had happened to Georges, and was only prevented by a sure knowledge of his resentment if she exposed herself and him in that way, yet she was able to tell herself with confidence that if the very worst had happened, it would have got known—would have filtered out through the servants, through Masses announced in church, through mourning worn by the Baron and Madame. But there were no rumours, no horror-stricken whispers, no sign of black in Madame's dress or in what the Baron called his " sports " (indicating clothes of material that meant to be Scotch tweed, colour meant to be khaki, cut meant to be that of an English gentleman out shooting—but which failed at all points, as Frenchmen's clothes so often do). So far, so good.

There existed in Madeleine, as in so many women of those days, the queerest contradiction. Fearing daily and desperately the very worst—death to their loved man—they never could believe in it happening, often even when it did actually happen, as was usual in those years. Relieved, respited at least from the major anxiety —for Georges must be in hospital or depôt somewhere, and out of the fighting, Madeleine began to be a prey to a lesser—to know what had happened to him ? which led her curiosity to explore the unknown at least once a day.

*   *   *   *

Meanwhile, the war that had dealt her that private blow was gentle with her. The English kept on increasing. Seldom was the farm without its happy-go-lucky khaki crowd, whose slang, mixed with Indian words learned from old regular soldiers, and cheerful attempts at anglicized French phrases, Madeleine learned and used, as she learned the decorous politeness of the older officers, the shy good humour of the younger ones. Many a good sum did Blanquart pay her for billeting, many a neat bill did she receipt for anxious Mess Presidents. It was a queer education for a girl of her sort. At the convent school she had committed to memory certain facts about England and its people, not because they interested her, but because she soon discovered that it was easier to do lessons than to be punished for not doing them, and because her scheming mind knew by practice, if not by theory, that knowledge is power. And now she was having an object-lesson in very deed.

All the communes lying close to the line, whose population had been decimated by general mobilization, were being re-peopled by English-speaking men and women, in billets and horselines, rest-camp and hospitals, aerodromes and manœuvre grounds. Night after night she heard the winter darkness atremble with traffic on the road, and learned to know it as the sound of " caterpillars " (which she took to be the name of some new kind of road engine, and was not wrong) bringing up guns and yet more guns. This was interesting, comforting, profitable, there were no dull hours, no sense of danger, and plenty of money to be made. But it had an indirect effect which Madeleine saw clearly enough, if she did not trace the connection very closely. The more ships were torpedoed by German submarines, the fewer ships there were. The more English there were, the more ships were wanted. Therefore the still fewer ships to import foodstuffs. Therefore appeals from deputies, maires, publicists, parliamentarians of all sorts, praising, cajoling, inciting the " honest peasants " to grow more and more food. The greater waxed the importance of the question, the more the endless bargaining and speculating to which she and her father, instinctively prone, needed little encouragement.

Jerome Vanderlynden and all his sort—all backed up by wives and daughters more or less like Madeleine—hung on to their produce for better and better prices. Subsidies had to be granted, taxes eased, bounties promised, facilities given. Then they would go on and grow some more—and then hang out again for greater and greater benefits. Beet, haricots, potatoes, wheat, barley, oats, all served their turn. Flax doubled in price, and doubled again. Hops were worth their weight in gold. Chicory had to be the object of special legislation. The farmers learned slowly, but surely. There was no brisk, open " business as usual " propaganda—and no need for it. The dour old men, and quiet, careful women and girls, were not likely to miss the opportunity. The atmosphere was right. If death and disaster come to-morrow—" gather ye rosebuds while ye may." Gathering rosy thousand-franc notes is even better. And who would blame an old man with one son dead and one a prisoner, with his barn full of English soldiers who smoked pipes and set lighted candles among the straw as they wrote home, not to mention the ever-present possibility of shells—like all the farms Armentières way—or bombs—like all those toward St. Omer.

*   *   *   *

As a side issue, the social position of the peasant farmer began to improve. He had been accustomed to brief spells of flattery at election times—not to the wave of adulation that now engulfed him. He began to look the whole world in the face, and fear not any man. But many a man began, if not to fear him, at least to seek his good offices. Besides all the politicians, the contractors, the endless train of semi-public opportunists the War had created, the easy-going world of retired middle-aged people that are to be found in every French Department, suddenly discovered that the only way to remain easy-going was to get the farmer to befriend them. Everything from coals to chicken meal, from bread to cotton was being rationed. That facile plenty which is the basis of the French provincial middle class was threatened. Thus, as 1916 advanced, and the long sordid epic of Verdun began to string out its desperate incidents, the Baron Louis d'Archeville, walking round his shooting with the air of a child gazing at a birthday cake it has been forbidden to touch, bowler hat, " sports," camp-stool, all complete, stumped over the pavement of the yard, and found Madeleine putting her week's washing through the portable wringer.

Having it in his mind to ask for wooden logs, eggs, ham, and anthracite, he naturally began :

" Ah, good day, Madeleine, pretty as ever ! "

" Good day, Monsieur le Baron."

" And this brave Jerome, he goes well ? A glass of beer ? I shall not say no ! " He sat down on a wheelbarrow and waited for her to call her father.

Old Jerome came at Madeleine's cry of " Papa, kom ben t'haus ! " from picking over his seed potatoes.

Madeleine, who wanted the men out of the way, let it pass for politeness that she took the carafe of beer and two hastily washed glasses into the kitchen, swabbed the table and invited the Baron to place himself. She went back to her wringer, leaving the door into the scullery open. One never knew. She had kept her secret in her heart ever since her visit to the English hospital. She had no news, and had been able to think of no new way of getting even with the War, but she had forgotten nothing, forgiven nothing, renounced nothing.

Old Jerome, who, even a year before, would have stood in the Baron's presence until told to

be seated, now sat down beside his landlord
without apology.

The Baron did not remark on this, but said :
" Then, you have your farm all full of English ? "

" They do damage enormously."

" Very likely, but you have the right to be
paid ! "

" They pay, but they do damage all the same."

Old Jerome was not going to let go a possible
advantage.

The Baron, whose feelings against the English
had been cool from 1870 until Fashoda, then
violent until the idea of the Entente and its meaning had filtered into his unreceptive mind, had
just been reading propagandist literature, " The
English Effort',' and so forth, designed for just
such as he. Expanding with the new ideas he
had received, he reviewed the situation at some
length, dwelling on England's immense resources
of material, untouched reserves of men, all that
cheerful unknown which was so comforting in
face of unpleasant known facts of the growing
wastage of France.

Jerome added one remark born of the unaccustomed way money was now handed about. " Besides, they are rich ! " which led the Baron on
again, along the path pointed out by yet another
pamphlet he had been reading, on the subject of
the new war loan.

Much of the verbiage and all the argument was
lost on old Jerome. He was thinking of his sons

and poured out another glass for himself and the Baron. " It's a grievous business, this war," he sighed. " You must feel that as much as I."

The Baron did not miss the allusion, blinked a moment, for what is one to say to a man who has two sons, one of whom is dead and for ever gone, and the other a prisoner, with uncertain prospects. He concluded that the most comforting thing was to talk of his own son. Besides, he preferred to.

" At last we have news of Georges. He has written to us, you will never divine from whence ! "

He waited a moment, but old Jerome was not good at guessing. In the scullery the wringer was no longer creaking as it turned, and the splashing of water and the soft flop of the clothes into the tin pail had ceased.

" He has written from Monte Carlo. It seems that the army surgeons found he was making himself a bad chest, and sent him to the south for convalescence. He is being marked inapt for service, but he still wishes to do his part, and they will put him in this French Mission with the English Army as Officer-Interpreter. One day or another, we may see him here, if he is attached to a division that passes this way."

In the scullery Madeleine was standing over the wringer, allowing herself to smile ever so little. Within her breast her blood was dancing to the tune " I knew it, I knew it ! " Now, that terribly serious Georges of the day of mobilization that she did not understand and for whom she could do nothing would be changed back to the gay Georges (Monte Carlo, she had heard him speak of it, could see and hear him doing so now) that she did understand, and who would want her. The Baron was talking of other things now, of how the French would take it easy, and how the English would come in and finish the War. It was quite their turn. One had made sufficient sacrifices. Could Jerome let him have —this, that, and the other ? She paid little heed. Her father bargained a bit, then acquiesced. She thought it fitting, when the Baron rose to go, to come to the door of the kitchen and say :

" Au revoir, Monsieur le Baron.

" Au revoir, Madeleine, remain young and pretty, it is all one asks of you ! "

*　　*　　*　　*

She on her side asked little. She would get Georges back. She was sure now. The days might pass, nothing happen, no news come, but she was sure, sure as though he had written giving the date of his arrival.

Spring came—never more beautiful than in Flanders, where beauty can only exist on a basis of utility. It came shyly, a northern spring. The sodden greyness of the marshland winter on flat hedgeless fields gave way to cold and fitful sunshine that shone on rich young green everywhere, while the black dripping leaves of the elms in the dank pastures seemed blurred in vapour, that, upon examination, proved to be but a profusion of tiny light-coloured buds. And then something happened. It began happening so far away and so high up among the principalities and powers of this world that it was weeks before Madeleine felt its effects.

As the horrors of Verdun dragged on, the wastage that was obvious to so mediocre an observer as the Baron began to be acutely felt at the more sensitive Great Head-quarters. So much so that Great Head-quarters of France insisted to British Great Head-quarters that something must be done. British Great Headquarters, well groomed, well mannered, had a long way then still to go before it should shake off its slightly patronizing attitude towards its ally. It merely said that something should be done when it was ready. Great Head-quarters of France, doubting when that time would come to a people who had to be so well groomed and well mannered, insisted still harder. British Great Head-quarters replied good-humouredly, " Oh, very well then ! " It became known that there was to be a British offensive in the Somme. Gigantic rearrangements were necessary, and among the million schemes, orders and moves, was the establishment of Corps Head-quarters at Hondebecq. This necessitated a lot of room, and the mere fighting troops had to be pushed farther out. Thus Madeleine, one fine morning early in March, only just saved herself from dropping a saucepan of boiling soup. An officer-interpreter, in the uniform of the French Mission, had ridden into the yard. She knew the uniform well, had seen many such a one, but since the Baron's last visit it meant to her only one person. Her emotion, kept well under, was gone in a flash. She saw directly, as the officer dismounted, it was not Georges. He came from the new Corps Head-quarters to say that no more infantry would be billeted at the farm. Instead, she would be expected to house the Corps Salvage Officer.

Madeleine knew little and cared less as to what this might mean, except as it affected the work of the farm. She waited, and in a few days an elderly gentleman appeared who had the tall angular figure, whiskers, and prominent teeth of French caricatures of English people of the nineteenth century. With him came a gig, a motor-car, three riding horses, servant, groom, chauffeur and sundry dogs. He surveyed the room offered him coolly enough, had some alterations made in the position of bed and washstand, but warmed in his manner at once when he discovered, in the course of a few hours, that Madeleine could speak really resourceful if slangy English, and understood about his cold bath. He had had such difficulty, he told her, and the French were so dirty. Madeleine smiled (for he had passed her estimate for accommodation and cooking without a murmur) and took him under her wing. There was something about him that she dimly associated with what her father might have been, in totally different circumstances—a mixture of helplessness and partiality to herself. She mended his bed-socks and filled his india-rubber hot-water bottle almost with affection. He on his side would often say words which she took for endearment, in what he conceived to be French—was less trouble than the ever-changing battalion messes, and paid, in the long run, nearly as much. She was glad to have the barns freed from everlasting fear of fire, and to get them empty before the summer. The space which the Salvage required she had Blanquart measure up, and charged at the rate laid down in the billeting regulations. It came to nearly as much as housing infantry.

*　　　*　　　*　　　*

This old gentleman, by name Sir Montague Fryern, and his " salvage dump " were merely concrete evidence which slowly revealed to Madeleine what was going on. The idea of " salvage " had been imposed upon English fighting formations unwillingly, from somewhere high up and far off, some semi-political Olympus near Whitehall. Divisional and Corps Staffs knew better than to resist. They thought it silly and superfluous—the war was trouble enough, and already much too long and dangerous for the average regular soldier, without having to economize material as well. But, wise with eighteen months of such a war as they had never dreamed of, and hoped never to see again, they had found out that the way to deal with these mad ideas invented by people at home, was to acquiesce, and then to side-track them. So when pressed for the third time for reasons why they had not appointed a Salvage officer, the Corps Staff now functioning at Hondebecq looked at one another, and some one said jokingly, " Let's make old Fryern do the job ! "

The baronet had been almost a national joke. In 1914 dapper old gentlemen in London clubs had said :

" Heard about old Fryern ? "

" No ! "

" He's joined up as a private in the R.A.M.C."

Some one said it was to avoid commanding a battalion, some that it was to escape scandal or a writ, others that it was merely " just like old Fryern ! " In the course of a year he had become notorious for prolonging officers' convalescence with illicit drink, and the King, it was said, had insisted on his taking a commission. Too eccentric to be put in a responsible position, and insisting on not remaining in England, he had drifted about Divisional, and then Corps Head-quarters until this heaven-sent opportunity housed him in a suitable nook. A man of unexpected resource, no sooner had he understood what was required

73

of him than he began to gather at the Spanish
Farm the most miscellaneous collection of objects
ever seen together since Rabelais compiled his
immortal lists of omnium gatherum. A field-
gun, a motor-car, other people's servants, several
animals, French school books, Bosche pamphlets,
sewing machines, ploughs and tinned food ;
nothing came amiss to him. What good he did,
no one could say. Little of the stuff was re-
issued and served the purpose of economy, but
when Dignitaries from British Great Head-
quarters came down to see Corps Head-quarters
and said to its old friends : " I say, Charles, you
were awfully slack about that Salvage Order, you
know ! " the old friends were able to answer :

" Well, we aren't now ; you come and see old
Fryern's dump after lunch—say about three ! "

" What, old ' Chops ' Fryern ? "

" No other, I assure you ! " and so on.

*   *   *   *

It happened, only a week or so after Sir Montague's arrival at the farm, that a lorry stopped in
the yard. There was nothing unusual in that.
They did so at all hours of the day and most of
the night. The English, so wits said, fought on
rubber tyres. Old Jerome, leaning on his hoe,
type of primitive man drudging with his primitive
implement to wring a subsistence from inscrut-
able Nature, often stood to watch these powerful,
docile servants of a younger age, that could do the

work of ten men and four horses in half an hour. He was doing so now, and Madeleine, if she thought about it at all, thought like this : " Poor old father, he's making old bones ; it's the boys he misses," when she saw Jerome drop his hoe and run to the lorry to help out a woman with a shawl over her head.

In another moment Madeleine had no doubt. It was her sister Marie from Laventie. In a moment she was out. The men on the lorry, with the queer, dumb, unexpected kindliness of the poorer Englishman, were handing down Emilienne, Marie's little girl, in a sort of frozen stupor of cold and fright. Madeleine ran to take the child, while her father helped Marie, who seemed dazed, into the house. Round the kitchen stove, quickly stoked until the top shone red, Madeleine plied them with the inevitable coffee, and presently with slabs of staunch farm bread.

Jerome stood by, the mere helpless male in the face of calamity. It was he who said first :

" What is it, my girl ? "

At first Marie could only say, " O, my God ! " and rock herself. But presently, reviving under the influence of food and drink, and the still more potent surroundings of safety in that familiar, warm old kitchen, where she had grown up, began to tell of the daily increase in shelling and bombing. In her half-empty farm-house, with the glass long gone from its shuttered windows, and the machine-gun bullets in its walls, relics of the first engagement with the Germans in 1914, she had billeted some English Engineers. The sector had been quiet ever since Neuve Chapelle, a year before. Suddenly, as the English sat with her around the fire, the shell had come. It had fallen in the doorway of the farm and had flung half the house upon the soldiers. Marie, protected by the solid brick chimney-piece, as soon as she got her breath, had scrambled under the debris to the room where Emilienne was crying to her. The door was jammed by a fallen beam. Some soldiers had run from a neighbouring billet, had broken in the door and got the child out. How they had all tramped up the road, shells ahead, shells behind, shells falling each side, with the sky red and the air rocking with the English artillery retaliation, she could not tell. At last, at a dump of some sort the Engineers had put her on a lorry that had taken her to Strazeele. Farther than that they could not go ; it was the limit of their Corps area. Marie and Madeleine had been educated by the past eighteen months, and knew better than to expect a lorry to go outside its Corps area. So Marie had had to walk, with the child in her arms, to Caestre, where she had found, thank God ! plenty of lorries running back from railhead. On hearing her tale, an officer had allowed her to get into one that was going to Hondebecq, and she had easily persuaded the driver to go as far as Spanish Farm.

At this point there was a tap on the door, which was opened by a khaki-clad figure, with a sheepish face and unmistakable Cockney accent.

" Beg parding, mum, but 'ow's yer little gal ? "

" Give them something to take, they had been so——" she used the untranslatable word " gentil," for which " decent " is perhaps the nearest equivalent. But Marie meant what the word perhaps originally meant—human as against inhuman, civilized as against barbarous.

Madeleine took out mugs of coffee and rum, and was rewarded by a cheerful, " Thank ye, kindly, miss, and here's the very best ! "

Madeleine came back, stepping softly. Emilienne had sunk into a deep, heavy sleep, interrupted by twitching and muttering, in the chimney corner. Giving her a glance, Madeleine clasped her hands.

" O Marie, all your things ! The brass bedstead, the beer glasses, the clock ! "

Marie shook her head, tears ran down her face.

Above her, old Jerome, caring little for women's fallals, muttered : " Thank God, the little one was spared ! "

Like all other incidents of the War, there it was. Shells fell, something was destroyed. One went on as well as one could. That was the history of the past eighteen months, was to be the history of another two years and a half—just a perpetual narrow margin of human survival over all the disasters humanity could bring upon itself. Not that the Vanderlyndens took the large impersonal view. Marie and Emilienne slept most of that day. The next, they started in to work, in their varying capacities. The first thing Marie did was to spend a day, bribing lorry drivers and cajoling officers, to get back to Laventie and see what was left. The beetroot had been sold, the potatoes had gone with the horse and cart to Aunt Delobeau's near Bailleul, because for some time Marie had been unable to keep a man on the farm, and had worked it with such village women as had been stranded like herself by general mobilization, the Government being only too glad to leave them there, to cultivate almost under machine-gun fire, as long as they would. But since the fatal night, the gendarmerie had become nervous of the place, though the actual shelling had ceased. They would not allow her to sow the ground, and were moving the powers that watch over France to obtain an order of general evacuation of the commune, which they no longer desired to patrol. With difficulty she obtained permission to fetch away the seed and one or two agricultural implements. The dwelling-house had burnt out, for the split stove had flung its flaming coals on thatch and beams. She was spared the spectacle of inevitable looting by Allies, and on returning to the Spanish Farm, settled down into the position she had left, in 1910, to be married.

Outwardly, Madeleine acquiesced. Marie was the elder sister—eldest child, in fact—and had all the prestige of a married woman. She was also more purely peasant than Madeleine and easily jealous of her rights. Madeleine, since she had had Georges, had ceased to envy her sister. Now, losing Georges, she lost her secret comfort, and any satisfaction she may have drawn from being mistress of the house, brains of the farm. But Madeleine by long brooding on her secret fixed idea—Georges—had come to that point at which she accepted these outward superficial happenings, estimating their importance solely by the standard of that Fixed Idea. At first she was unable to see how the advent of Marie and Emilienne affected her reconquest of Georges.

*   *   *   *

She was soon to learn.

Marie, for a few days preoccupied with herself, startled by what had happened, and rather grateful for home and shelter, soon emerged from that numbed state which, medically the result of concussion, is one of the first universal symptoms of shell-shock. She began to be masterful and critical of Madeleine's former management. She had run two messes for the Engineers in her small Lys valley house, with far less scope than the Spanish Farm afforded. Madeleine pointed out that she had done all that, and would have continued but for movements of troops over which she had no control. Marie agreed, sighing for the busy days when she had cooked and done for

79

three officers, and scores of hungry men, just out or just going into the trenches, to whom Emilienne had sold chocolate, cigarettes, writing paper and candles to great advantage. Perhaps also she was jealous of Madeleine, of the younger girl's smarter looks, less peasant-like and matronly than her own, of her untouched good luck during the long anxiety of the war, for, like all the world, Marie knew nothing of the secret about Georges. But things kept happening. Presently the right thing happened.

Podevin, who kept the " Lion of Flanders " inn, on the Grand' Place of Hondebecq, gave up. He had made money, of course, especially latterly since Corps Head-quarters had been in the village, and had enabled him to open a dining-room for officers. But, like so many, he had lost his only son at Verdun, and, heartbroken, cared no longer even to amass wealth. The long, biscuit-coloured house, with its two storeys and old steep-tiled roof was for sale. Marie saw the notice and told Madeleine at once :

" There's your chance ! "

Madeleine took her habitual half-minute of reflection, trying this new idea against her Fixed Idea. They suited marvellously. Why had she not thought of it before ? (The true answer was that she was not sufficiently imaginative.) She saw now that in taking the " Lion of Flanders " she would be placing herself exactly where Georges must come if his division were moved this way, which was sure to happen sooner or later. And the whole thing was so natural that he would never be able to make her the one reproach she feared so much—of running after him and making their liaison obvious.

The two women went to see Podevin together, before they told old Jerome. Podevin could only say, " I've lost my son—let me alone ! "

They fetched in Blanquart, as was usual in such cases. The grizzled schoolmaster arranged it. Madeleine pretended to be shocked at the price, standing in Blanquart's little parlour, with the sound of the school classes grinding out the morning lesson like some gigantic gramophone gone mad, just through the wall. But secretly she nudged Marie. The worst was over. The price named was well within what she kept about her in the house in notes. She would not have to draw on the savings bank at Hazebrouck. That made all the difference in tackling her father. But when the two daughters broached the subject that evening, he acquiesced. It would be a good business, he said. Madeleine, who had never forgotten how he had, all unasked, fetched Lieutenant Skene to help her on the day of the visit to the hospital, wondered how much her father guessed of her secret. Something, surely. But it was just the sort of subject on which neither of them could speak to each other. So all she said was, " You know, you're a good father ! "

*   *   *   *

THE SPANISH FARM

The War, that had wounded her so deeply where she was most vulnerable, was kind to her in little things. No sooner was she installed in the "Lion of Flanders," and had got together some three or four village women who had young families or other domestic ties that had made them anxious to get any work they could within a hundred yards of their doors, while forbidding them to go out for the day to the farms that needed them, than Corps Head-quarters arranged a Horse Show, a form of amusement that became very fashionable in the B.E.F. as the years went on. Officially, it was inaugurated to keep drivers and orderlies up to their work. Subconsciously it indulged that national failing, love of horses and open air, so curious in a town-bred nation. Madeleine, of course, paid no more heed to this than she did to any other of the curious foibles of those incomprehensible English, until she found that most of the officers of three divisions would be in the village nearly all day for this function, many of them ten miles from their own messes, and glad enough to find a decent meal. She laid her plans and purchased wisely and well. Then, only two days before the festival, Sir Montague offered to take her to the show. She thought for half a minute, and accepted, almost jubilantly.

*　　　*　　　*　　　*

She was feeling the long strain, however much she concealed it with silent composure. And, as with all women in her particular "irregular" position, she had begun to hug the golden illusion that goes with it, and makes it for some so possible to bear. She had lost Georges; he was gone from her side, in spite of her, pulled away by something he held dearer. He had not come back, not written. She could not, dare not if she could, go or write to him. But she still believed, as all such women do, "Oh, if I could only see him!" She still nourished that pathetic faith, still believed that if only she could stand face to face with him, things would be again as they had been. There was, however, that terrible danger haunting the attempt to get face to face with him. He might think or feel she was following him. That, she knew, would be fatal. In Sir Montague, therefore, she saw a heaven-sent angel. Too old, too cranky, too well known (as she had soon discovered) to be the object of scandal regarding her, he would take her under his wing and she would be at the Horse Show, to be seen. Georges, if he were there, would see her. That was the safest. Once he saw her she had perfect confidence in herself. She would know instinctively, would not look, not she. But she would will it, and he would have to come. She recognized clearly enough now, how simply, passively, unconsciously she had made their first hour alone together, when she had given herself, in the shelter at the Kruysabel. She had only to do it again. This also comforted her, for she was not original.

She accepted Sir Montague's invitation graciously, and took care to look her best on the day.

*　　*　　*　　*

The day came, and she was ready. Radiant with health, wishing to be dressed in her own way, in a mixture of country primness and the English style she secretly admired (coat and skirt and all-weather hat), she had compromised at the skirt of her pigeon-grey saxony costume, a cream-coloured blouse that left her elbows and neck bare, with nothing on her head but her own crisp dark hair. Thus adorned, she esteemed herself as nearly a lady (i.e. a person who does no work) as she had any need to be, while not too far removed from the mistress of the " Lion of Flanders."

Before Sir Montague came to fetch her, as she was perfecting her arrangements at her restaurant, Lieutenant Skene appeared with a gunner officer she did not like, who was obviously joking about her. She greeted her friend kindly, in English, and ignored the other. She was flattered to see that the lieutenant was evidently taking her part, trying to make the other behave, looking very sheepish and funny as he clumsily concealed his obvious feeling for her. They reserved a table and went away. Sir Montague was punctual and she stepped up into the gig with the ease of one who has always had to use her limbs. She was elated. Men looked after her. The sun shone. In the queer gauche Flemish springtime, buds and shoots hung stiffly in the still air like heraldic emblems. A band was playing, people were moving about. Everything whipped her excitement. They drove on to Verbaere's big pasture, behind the mill, and put the gig with the other vehicles, all parked and stewarded as on an English race-course. Sir Montague had a way of arching his elbow, twirling his whip, and fetching a great circle before he brought his conveyance to a standstill that caused, she noticed, much laughter, and the beginnings of a cheer.

He handed her into a rough enclosure, where English nurses in grey and red and white coifs, Canadian nurses in blue and scarlet, Australian sisters in grey-brown, fine big girls in their mannish hats, mixed with a sprinkling of the wives of local maires and notaries, small French officialdom and business circles. Some of these ignored Madeleine, perhaps did not know her, but the brewer's wife from the next village, invited by the A.S.C. colonel billeted on her, gave a cheery " Good day, Madeleine," that would have put anyone at ease. But Madeleine was already at her ease. She saw she was getting more attention than any other woman on the ground. She had dressed just right, awakened none of the submerged sensibilities of those queer English. That and a glance at the lovely horses, shining, prancing, bobbing head and floating tail—for she loved fine animals—was all she cared to notice before she settled herself, eyes straight to the front, and put out all her feelers for the one purpose for which she had come. Poor Madeleine, no one had bothered to tell her that there were already over fifty English divisions in France, and among the men before her she stood one chance in seventeen of finding Georges. They passed about her, Easthamptons, Lincolns, Norfolks, A.S.C., R.A.M.C., R.A.F., gunners, Engineers, French Mission in blue and strawberry, wonderful staff people, in khaki and leather so perfect that it outshone all the bright colours of the French. She took it all in, tried to sort it out, mused over it, especially the name " Lincoln," which, like all French people, she was incapable of pronouncing. She could form no idea of which group was the likeliest to be Georges', glanced over the face and figures of the French Mission officers. More than any close examination, her instinct told her, Georges was not there. A sort of numbness came over her, she felt it almost like a physical sensation. It seemed to be in her legs. She fought against it, would not give in to it. Then, all of a sudden, too suddenly for her strong, resolute, unimaginative nature, she did give in.

The corps officials had hardly begun judging the riding-horses when she slipped from her place, round behind the stand, out between the wagon-teams, waiting their turn, with cunning drivers of all arms surreptitiously dabbing metal and leather with handkerchiefs, looking stolidly

over the exhibits they belonged to, speaking
gently to them in low voices. She found a well-
known gap in the hedge and got through into the
back lane that ran towards Verbaere's mill.
Up this, picking her way in the mud to save her
best boots, she came into the village by the yard
of the " Lion of Flanders." The numbness was
gone from her legs. Instead, her pulse beat in
her temples so loud that she hardly heard the
band playing " Watch your Step," and the cheering as the riding-horses, classed by the judges,
filed round the ring, and out.

*   *   *   *

She let herself into the " Lion of Flanders "
by the back door, which she shut with a clang,
She looked magnificent and just a bit desperate,
so that, of her waiting-women, one said to another.
" She's in fine fettle this morning, our young
patronne ! " But she was not the woman to do
the more ordinary desperate things. No—yes.
A stitch of her close-sewn self-control had parted.
She was not going to stand it. Her mental attitude contained nothing of an English suffragette's
logical, theoretical stand upon " rights." Her
pride was hurt. Georges was Georges, dearer
than life, but there now glimmered behind him
something dearer than that—her dignity, what
was due to her—Herself, of course, in reality.
She swept a glance round the neat, well-laid
tables, sniffed the redolent preparation of the

kitchen. She—dragged about behind a man's shadow that ever eluded her ! Of course, her feeling was incoherent, ill-defined, just a sense of resentment against something she did not trouble to identify, but it was there. Reckless, she went down the stone steps into the cellar. Among the casks of weak beer and carefully " lengthened " wine she had taken over from Podevin, was a bottle marked " Chambertin," which she recognized as an oversight. It was good stuff. She had hidden it with the English Expeditionary Force canteen whisky and the rum she had got out of Sir Montague. Now her thought was, " They shan't have it, those English ! " She took it up, glanced at the coating of the bottle neck, and mounted the stairs with it.

" Berthe," she cried—she had borrowed the girl from the farm for the day—" four glasses and some bread ! "

Putting on her black alpaca apron, she pulled the cork, holding the bottle steady with a firm wrist, and poured out. Raising her glass, she said to them : " I give you that ! " and drank amid a murmur of " Thank you, Madeleine." Outside the services of the Church, the only ceremonial she had ever been taught to observe was connected with good wine. The Chambertin lived up to her gesture, with its broad, almost coarse flavour, a legend among the frugal Flemish at their rare feasts. Outwardly, what she did was just a bit of unexpected generosity toward

four employees who could do with a heartening
for the twelve hours' hard work that lay ahead of
them, from which she intended to draw handsome
profit. Within her heart it was, unconsciously,
perhaps, almost a sacramental act, the opening of
a new life. The blood in her was beating out the
time, " I won't stand it any longer ! "

*   *   *   *

The square-footed beakers, of the sort which
would be called " rummers " in England, were
empty, the substantial finger-pieces munched and
swallowed, before there came the sound of spurred
boots on the cobbles and the clients began to
arrive. First two Canadian majors with the
Maire came to claim the table they had reserved,
and found it kept for them, the coarse napkins
starched, the heavy cutlery and glass in place, and
Madeleine with her best smile and hardly a trace
of accent asking : " What would you like for
lunch ? " at which the Maire stared. Behind
them trooped others. The room was soon full,
the glass windows clouded with steam, the noise
of conversation and table-ware deafening.

Imperturbable, Madeleine moved among it.
The waiting may have been amateur. The cooking was thorough in the solid Flemish fashion. At
least, no one was left staring at an empty plate or
glass. Madeleine, a smile for every one, and a
glib English explanation for every difficulty, used
the mental arithmetic she had learnt at the market,

in calculating bills. Her clients went off with heightened colour and laughing voices, amid trails of tobacco smoke. Manfully, Madeleine and her staff cleared the place, fed themselves and washed up. They had only got the tables reset before that extraordinary meal "afternoon tea" was demanded of them. Madeleine was equal to the occasion. It might be a foolish custom, but it paid. And this merged into dinner, long and heavy as is the Flemish custom. Younger officers, and especially those down from the line, were getting boisterous, rude. She had to put up with many a clumsy joke, many a suggestion. She was too busy and too utterly unafraid to care. One thing did rather amuse her. At the table he had reserved for his party, the Lieutenant Skene was following her with his eyes and ears, and getting so cross at the treatment she was receiving. At length, just as it was all becoming too boisterous, and the younger officers were getting out of hand, suddenly, from the little private room that had been reserved for Brigadier-General Devlin and his friends, came the sound of a piano—the good piano she had got from the château. Not musical, and unwilling to spend time over such trifles, she was forced to stop and listen. It was Chopin, some one said. It had the most extraordinary effect. General Devlin and the officer who had been playing went away. The rest of the crowd in the big room went also, the rowdiness gone from them, subdued, seduced from their daily selves by the music. On Madeleine the effect was strongest. Wrought up by the events of the day and by sheer fatigue (she had been on her feet twelve hours), the lovely stuff, that could not act on her unreceptive spirit, antipathetic to it, merely saddened her. After another laborious wash up, she dismissed her helpers, locked the house and started for home. It was past midnight, and the day that had been so fine left a dark windy night, promising rain before morning. As she trod the pavé of the grand'route and the earth of the farm road, she felt miserable and beaten. It was easy enough to say, "I won't stand it!" Like so many other people, she found it so difficult to do. How not to stand and what not to stand? Forget Georges? Could she? Would she if she could? Go and find him, and thus make him forget her? Which?

*   *   *   *

The corps did not have a horse show every day, but the one just passed had been a good advertisement for the "Lion of Flanders," and Madeleine began to do a quiet, regular business in luncheons and teas for the officers that incessantly circled round and about Corps Headquarters. To be busy soothed her feeling of helplessness, and the necessity for this soothing kept her polite, skilful, attentive. Some weeks passed, and then again, far away, and high up, undreamed of by her, things began to happen.

THE SPANISH FARM

The English offensive in the Somme, heralded
as a great victory, had in reality made infinitesimal
gains at the cost of enormous loss. The British
Great Head-quarters, then still functioning in
complete disunity with Great Head-quarters of
France, and often in good-humoured disregard of
the advice given it, went on butting, like an obstinate ram, at the same place. This, though it
surprised the Germans more than the most subtle
strategy would have done, cost the lives of many a
thousand English soldiers. It was necessary to
economize and economize again. The reserve
corps would have to disappear, the line northward
be more sparsely held. Here the long chain of
action and reaction touched Madeleine.

For two days she was feverishly busy, officers
wanting meals at all hours in great numbers. On
the third morning, as she came down in the blaze
of July seven-o'clock weather, she found a long
string of lorries, grinding and jolting, behind
them officers' servants with led horses, mess-carts,
police. They went. A silence as of peace-time
settled on the remote Flemish village, lost in the
undulating fertile plateau between Dunkirk and
Lille. Twenty kilometres eastward was the line,
full of troops. Twenty kilometres west were the
great manœuvre areas where men learned to kill
and not be killed more and more scientifically.
At Hondebecq, nothing. It took nearly a week
to convince Madeleine, who was not interested in
the more general aspects of the War. She was

not really convinced until the Baron walked into her empty dining-room.

" Good day, Madeleine, you have lost all your clients."

Looking up from her knitting, she said gravely:

" It seems so ! " But secretly she now believed it. If it were not true he would not have come. He disliked the crowd of junior officers who joked about his beard.

What was to be done ? Not retain an empty restaurant where no one ever came. She saw enough at home in the evenings to know that Marie was firmly settled in, and didn't want her. The situation was beyond her. Her practical mind focussed on the immediate was baffled. But things went on happening and once again the long arm of chance touched her.

It was about a fortnight after Hondebecq had been plunged in its unnatural silence. She was going home in the long July twilight. She no longer waited to serve late dinners, her only customers being occasional passing troops during the day. No local people used the " Lion of Flanders," it was essentially an English restaurant. She was stopped at the level-crossing by the evening train from Calais going southward. As the smoke and noise faded away, she ran into Blanquart, the schoolmaster and communal secretary, stumbling over the platform-edging, wiping his eyes. The sight of that familiar figure in tears gave her pause.

"Why, Monsieur Blanquart, what is it?"

"It is my little Cécile!"

"What has she got, Cécile?"

Monsieur Blanquart blew his nose and said:
"I ought not to complain. She was a good girl.
Naturally she has got a good job."

"What job has she got? Where has she gone,
then?"

"But to Amiens! You haven't seen the
discourse of M. Paul Deschanel on the Recruit-
ment of Women? It is hanging in the Mairie
if that gives you any pleasure."

Madeleine, grey-eyed, her mouth a straight
line, her hands crossed over the little bag that
contained the day's takings, stared at him between
the eyes a full half-minute. Then she said:
"Ah, I sympathize with you. Good evening,
Monsieur Blanquart."

She went away thinking, and thought to some
effect.

*   *   *   *

First, a refugee Belgian family was installed in
the derelict "Lion of Flanders," where they all
lived in the dining-room round the stove, boarded
up the big windows, and got jobs in the village.
Then Madeleine was seen in earnest consultation
with Blanquart. Finally it was known that she
had got a job in a Government office at Amiens,
from which the men had just been combed out.

"Tiens!" said the gossips. "Cécile Blan-

quart first, now Madeleine Vanderlynden. Who
next ? "

The formalities took a week. Then Madeleine emerged with the papers of her appointment
in her hands. She went first to the " Lion of
Flanders " and told the refugee family in no
equivocal terms, how, when and where to pay
their rent to Marie. Leaving them in a state of
guttural exclamation, half gratefulness, half appre-
hension, she turned for a moment into the church,
and stood by the high-backed prie-Dieu that bore
the initials V.D.—Vanderlynden-Delplace—staring at the gimcrack ornaments of the altar, the
eternal childish innocence of the Catholic Church
decoration. Old Justine Schact was fidgeting
about her verger's duties. Birds scuffled in the
belfry as the chimes played their verse and a half
of hymn tune that marked the quarter hour.

Madeleine's lips, set by habit to utter a prayer
in those surroundings, formed something like
this : " Saint Madeleine, out of your divine pity,
grant me that I may see him, then it will be all
right ! " Her lips ceased to move. In her un-
bowed head, her steady eyes took on the gleam of
frosted marsh-pools. She squared her fine shoulders and clasped her large, capable hands on the
chair-back. She might have been an allegory of
indomitable Flanders. There was no mistaking
the glance she bent on the altar. It said, " Saint
Madeleine, if you don't . . ." But the threat
was never articulated. She turned and walked

out, erect and sure-footed. At the farm she told
her father what time to put the horse in, and when
it came, appeared from her room, her canvas-
covered wooden box locked and corded. She
made her adieu thus shortly :

"Good-bye, Marie, what luck you came. I
can go with a tranquil heart. Berthe will help
you well. Good-bye, Berthe. Good-bye, Emilienne, I will send you a pretty postcard !" To
the old house in which she and her father, and no
one knows how many ancestors had been born,
in which her mother had died, not a look. Either
it was too familiar, or simply did not appeal to her.
To the Kruysabel where she had known her brief
hours of bliss—not a look. She was going to
something better. Or perhaps, in her narrow
personal way, she felt that these things were part
of her, and that, so far as they existed, they went
with her.

At the station, standing beside her box as the
train came in, she turned with real affection to her
father, probably the one being in the world she
thoroughly understood and sympathized with.
But she only said, "Au revoir, Father," and he
only replied, "Au revoir, my girl." Then
with a hoist of strong arms and legs, she was into
the train, after which the old man stood a moment,
staring. But she was already settling herself in
her place, taking stock of her neighbours, girding
herself for her new campaign.

PART II
"ON LES AURA"

" *On les aura* "

MADELEINE went to Amiens, but it hardly describes what happened to say that she went by herself without other companion than chance fellow-travellers, for, in her, there entered the capital of Northern France more than a single Flemish girl. She took up with her, all about her, an atmosphere of the frontier, of staunch Flanders, of the Spanish Farm. Countrified she might be, certainly a stranger, but there was nothing callow or helpless about her. She showed that maturity that connoisseurs of wine mean when they speak of " body." Generations, a whole race, living in one way, confronted century after century with much the same environments, had prepared that quality in her, which led no one to wonder at or pity her. Had there been any Society for the Protection of Young Girls at the station at Amiens, it would not have considered her a " case," as she swung down on to the platform, produced her ticket and papers, and bargained with an old man with a barrow to take her box—a bargain she struck much to her advantage by shouldering the said box and starting to carry it herself.

The Amiens to which Madeleine went was the Amiens of mid-war—that is to say, a general manufacturing town of eighty thousand people, provincial, antiquated as such towns can be only in France—which town, plunged into European war, had seen the Germans march through its streets. It was now reserve railhead, camping-ground, last-civilized-spot for the avalanches of reinforcements the English were pouring into the line. Most of the French who fought beside them in that northern sector had to pass through it. Madeleine had not been able to calculate with any nicety how her move had increased her chances of meeting Georges, but she got as far as beginning to understand what the Baron had meant by the " English effort," the immensity of that Volunteer Army, the constant watching and waiting that would be necessary to find Georges among the hundreds of French Mission officers that went with it. But like all vague steps, the one that she had taken was comforting because of its novelty, its unplumbed depths of possibility. Once cut adrift from home, and having suppressed a tiny shyness, rising in the throat, she flung herself into the new life with gusto. She was not wholly ignorant of towns, had been to Hazebrouck and St. Omer, to Dunkirk even, once, and was ready as any country-grown girl to fall under the spell of town life and strive desperately to look as if she had always lived it.

* * * *

Her job was in one of those Government

Departments, whose staff, depleted by general mobilization, and further by repeated "combing-out," hardly sufficed to keep going that multiplicity of printed forms by which France is governed. She wrote a good hand, having acquired that art at a convent school where it, at least, was not reckoned among the subversive sciences. Perhaps she dimly saw in the power to write and read one of the advantages that such as she possessed over the less lucky. Handwriting, at any rate, was no difficulty. Figures she handled with respect, almost with appetite. As the first newness of the life thawed and broke before her, she began to prepare herself to take the lead in the office, as she had taken it at the farm. By the time August was turning into September, she almost smiled as she took her week's money. She would not have paid Berthe so much for doing such a job. Eight to twelve and two to six seemed to her a ridiculously light day. The heat of the town was sometimes oppressive, but the office, about the ill-kept state of which she grimaced to herself, was on the north side of one of those rococo barrack-like buildings that link the architecture of the chef-lieux of Northern France to that of Mediterranean civilization. That is, it had the dank chill of a tomb. She survived. As for the life in general, her iron health stood it well. She missed the air and exercise, but her diet was not full enough to allow her to fatten. She had been welcomed, of course,

by Cécile Blanquart, and taken, not without a
shade of kindly patronage, to lodge with the aunt
who sheltered Cécile. The aunt was one of
those widows of the small official class who seemed
to have disappeared from England since Dickens.
She was poorer, prouder, more impossibly ugly
and mean than anything surviving to us. She
would have housed Madeleine, had not each of
her tiny rooms already contained two people at
least. Clinging to any ha'pence that were to be
had, she arranged that the new-comer should dine
at the frugal common table she kept, and sleep a
few streets away in the third-floor attic over the
pork butcher's. Madeleine appeared to her what
is called in France " sérieuse." To Madeleine,
the arrangement appeared nothing short of
heaven sent.

She had applied herself to her job. She had
put out all her most feminine sensibilities to catch
the right note in dress and looks, for she was
nothing if not conventional. But in her heart
she was simply passing the days and waiting her
chance to find Georges. As she did her work,
altered and supplemented her clothes, took little
evening walks or visited the cinema with the
other girls, to all appearance just a strapping country cousin fitting herself into new surroundings,
she was, all the time, vigilant, relentless. She
drew the others down to the station on the pretext
of buying a paper at the hour the troop trains
passed or stopped. She preferred for her small

needs the shops that fronted the well-known
officers' restaurant, for Georges, she knew,
would do himself well if he had the chance.   As
to what exactly she would say or do if she saw
him she was not the girl to wonder.   She had
perfect faith in her illusion—just to see him face
to face, anyhow, anywhere.

*   *   *   *

Her companions with whom she worked, ate,
and spent her evenings, did not annoy her.
That is as much as she felt about them.   Although only a year or so her juniors, there was
nothing about them to excite her jealousy or even
her respect.   As she listened to them, making
little muddles over their jobs, giving way to small
passions and routine indispositions, chattering
with affected solemnity or secrecy of their opin-
ions, hopes, fears—above all of their love affairs—
she almost smiled.   She put more of herself into
even the purchase of hairpins than they did into
their liaisons.   Not that she was more generous
or less acquisitive than they, but simply because
there was more of her.   She had known real
work, hard bargains, the utter depth of passion—
things undreamed of in their little world of petty
officialdom and shop-assistantship.   Even the
country girls like Cécile stood mentally where
she, Madeleine, had not done since her mother
died.   Probably her principal minor preoccu-

pation (as distinct from her one great secret preoccupation) was the size of her body. She was half a head taller and much more substantial than most of them. She knew she was dressing herself right, sombre colours, good material and cut, little or no ornament—but her hands and feet gave her some anxious moments, they seemed so big. She gave considerable attention to her hands, using every means she could hear of to whiten them, and manicuring them elaborately, bringing to the work much patience and sense and no imagination. For her feet, she simply bought the best she could afford, not attempting to pinch them, relying on her strong ankles, straight back, and developed hips to keep her extremities in proportion. She was right. Men turned to look at her often enough and never with the superior, amused eye that she saw bent on her companions. She did not consciously care whether men looked or not, but there was just that comfort in it that she could tell that she was interpreting this strange new world rightly. Had she but known, she possessed two of the greatest advantages over most of the women in those surroundings—radiant health, that brightened her glance, polished her skin, burnished her hair—and, in spite of her quiet clothes and steady eyes, an air of independence of which she was probably unconscious, but which was far more attractive than the air of facile complicity with male patronage that many girls wore. Like all advantages, these carried with them their own inconvenience, as she soon discovered.

*   *   *   *

Among Aunt Blanquart's lodgers were men, too weedy or too well protected to have been mobilized. They functioned on the railway, or some other public service, she did not care what, with coloured brassards on their arms. She had paid no heed to them, secure in the fatal confidence of a strong nature, merely getting out of them anything they knew about the movements of troops, feigning the fatuous gossiping curiosity that was common enough. She was so immersed in her Fixed Idea that she was astonished when the more pimply of them slipped past Aunt Blanquart's semi-official vigilance, as she was going home to her room, and following her, proposed, " Suppose we take a little walk, as the English say ! "

Madeleine turned on him a freezing stare :
" What for ? " she demanded, standing her ground.

The pimply-faced one faded back into the house, muttering excuses, only to confide in his friends later that Madeleine was a " rosse," " an awkward beast," as one should say.

Then again, when the skull-capped old gentleman who controlled her room went sick, the worried head of the department came across to Madeleine naturally with : " Give out the work

to the room, while this old Do-nothing is away,
will you ? "

She did the distribution of the endless sched-
ules, minutes and circulars deftly enough, and
corrected the errors with a firm hand.   It took
far less thought than most of her days at the farm.
When the " old Do-nothing " returned, skull-
capped, pallid, smelling of lozenges, she met him
with : " I have done " so and so, and " you
will find this " there and that " under the paper
weight ! " etc., going quietly back to her desk.
At night he lingered, and was left alone with her,
because she was never in such a hurry as the
others to crowd downstairs, squabble in the lobby
over the inadequate space allowed for dressing
oneself for the walk home.   She turned and
stared as he asked her to dine with him.

An idea—one of her rare, slowly born ideas—
had come to being in her head.   In her serious-
ness she hardly noticed that he had taken it for
granted that she would go with him.   But she
almost smiled when he began to detail his little
plan.   She, who had known not merely trials of
cunning with Belgian horse dealers and hop merchants, but desperate evasion and deceit to meet
Georges in the Kruysabel, agreed to pretend to
Aunt Blanquart that she had a headache, and to
meet this old man at the corner of the street.
Fortunately it was dark at the hour named—dark
with that war-time darkness of a town within the
bombing area.   She had a difficulty to recognize

him in the crowd——and a great temptation to help
his shuffling steps. She felt a sort of charity
towards him, an inclination to take his arm and
help him——a feeling which increased as she saw
what careful plans he had laid. He did not take
her to a restaurant, where the unequal couple
they made would certainly have been the object of
more or less concealed amusement, but to the
back sitting-room of an old servant of his, who
was now caretaker at a big shop. It was discreet,
cosy. The cooking was good, the dinner ample,
chosen from the more easily digested dishes.
She was so touched by his evident enjoyment——
though she had her own quiet confidence in her
desirability——and by his desire to give her a good
time——and things had been rather thin since
mobilization——that the only tyranny she practised
on him was to make him send out for a bottle of
Burgundy; the pale sweet wines he offered seemed
to her below the occasion.

There was no awkwardness during the meal,
for she asked prudent, calculated questions——who
really moved, housed and regulated the flow of
troops——did he know the numbers or composition
of the English divisions——all the small details
most Frenchwomen——utterly innocent of spying
——asked eternally out of sheer curiosity and inter-
feringness. And when they had done eating she
had to put up with the demonstrations that men
make, who have either not had their fill in middle
life, or who have come to regard it as a necessity

not to be foregone. She had found that he did possess information and perhaps connections that might be useful to her Fixed Idea, and tolerated his attempts to solace his waning instincts, until, hearing the hour chime, she shook herself free, put herself tidy, and left him to find his way home —only, because he might be useful and sounded disappointed, she murmured, "Another time," at the door. Once in the street, she stepped briskly home, arrived at the door of her lodging about the usual hour of her return from Aunt Blanquart's, and went up to bed. She was plotting and scheming busily and had already forgotten her entertainer as though he had never existed.

*　　*　　*　　*

Indeed, he might have saved himself that trouble. In that last week of September, just as she was beginning to feel no more strange as a government clerk in Amiens than she had felt as a farmer's daughter in Hondebecq, there spread through the minor French circles the news of a further English offensive. From what source it came and how it took shape no one will ever know, but the perpetual hungry curiosity of the sort of people among whom Madeleine now lived, was suddenly glutted with the news that there was to be an offensive, and that the Prince of Wales was taking part. This set flame to the French imagination, among whose republican embers a royalist spark has ever glowed.

108

"ON LES AURA"

To Madeleine, whose restricted imagination conjured up some long defile of troops through the cobbled streets, led by a fair-haired English boy, the news seemed of great promise. Georges was certain to be there. She saw him, accurately enough, in the blue and strawberry of the French Mission, riding in the cavalcade. She got a day off—her old man was "complaisant," as the French say, and she found herself with a whole day on her hands, an equinoctial day of chill draughts and paling sunshine, of fluttering leaves and a stir in the blood.

She had tried to get some idea as to when and where the troops would pass, but all that she could gather was that the English police had been doubled. This only endorsed her preconceived notion of a parade through the town. She rose in good time and dressed herself carefully—in sombre colours, in coat and skirt, inclining rather to the English model, implacably neat, well-buttoned, without a spot of bright colour or a trace of expression on her face. She went out and down to the station, bought a paper, lingered about, tried to feel what was going on. The streets were crowded, and as she was seldom about at this hour she drew comfort from the fact. It was of course the usual crowd of the nearest town behind the line of an offensive, men of all ranks going and coming on leave, base and line-of-communication people, young officers with a day off, grizzled officers' servants sent in from the innumerable camps for shopping. There were English, of north country and south country, London and Liverpool, Welsh, Scotch, Irish, Channel Isles. There were Canadians talking Yankee, Anglo-Indians, in wonderful blouses with mailed shoulder-straps, tall gaunt Australians, fresh-faced New Zealanders, swarthy or tanned English South Americans, South Africans and Naval details. More than once she was stared at, twice spoken to, once followed. If the Prince of Wales did pass down that street, it was in one of those fleet Vauxhall cars, with red-capped staff officers. There was no cheering, no procession, nothing of the crude, out-of-date spectacle that would have delighted and encouraged her. By one o'clock she was desperately hungry and tired, and burning with a sort of spiritual fever.

She did not give up, however. Partly faithful, partly merely obstinate, she stuck to her furtive prowling, keeping ever closer to the well-known Restaurant "à la Paysanne Flamande." She knew her Georges. A thousand accidents might take him into this or that street, by rail or car, on horseback or on foot, but, between noon and two o'clock, there was no possible error, Georges would be sitting before the best-laid table he could find, napkin tucked into his buttonhole, saying he had the hunger of a wolf, making caustic fun of the bill of fare, and standing no nonsense with the waiter. The celebrated restaurant, entirely

a creation of the War, before which it had led a
struggling existence dependent on a billiard-table
and a mixed clientêle, presented a glass swing-
door between two large plate-glass windows, protected by round iron tables and chairs set among
desolate shrubs in boxes. The door opened into
a little-used café-lounge ; the eating-room had
replaced the billiard-table on the raised portion
of the floor up four steps at the back. Thus the
public in the street could see the legs and half the
bodies of the diners, but not their faces. Outside, a great sign-board, swung English-fashion
on a bracket, depicted an alleged Flemish peasant-
woman, in national costume, with international
features, and the immemorial vulgarity of such
efforts. Madeleine never even guessed that the
square of brilliant paint was an allegorical representation of herself, and would have been much
astonished to have been told so.

Two o'clock struck, and half-past, and suddenly
she had a physical qualm. What was it ? She
realized she was faint with hunger. Together
with the bodily emptiness and dizziness, there
rose in her a bitter wave of disgust and disillusionment. For the second time she set her teeth.
She would not stand it. Careless of the fact that
she was doing what was only done by women of a
sort she despised, because she considered they
were driving a dangerous, badly paid trade, she
pushed open the door, walked steadily into the
café, and sat down just as the tables were begin-

ning to go round. It was partly want of food, as she told herself, but partly, if she had admitted it, the moisture of desperate vexation in her eyes. She ordered a café crême of an unwilling waiter, who did not want French people there, in such a way that he brought it, at once, and properly done. The scalding sips soon revived her. She began to think, if thinking it can be called. Rather she just sat and felt. She felt the French equivalents of " I'm fed up with this "—" I'm going to put an end to it "—whatever It exactly was. Then less articulately she just felt sore. It was not in her to feel passively sore, but how to express her feeling by activity she could not see, at the moment.

*   *   *   *

The souls of women come, perhaps rather more often than those of men, to steep places down which the least touch will cause them to hurl themselves. Madeleine had been hanging on some such edge ever since the day of the Horse Show. It needed but the stroke of a feather to send her over.

Her trance was broken by the sound of field-boots on the steps that led down from the dining-room. Two officers were passing to the door, middle-aged junior officers of infantry or artillery, with cleaned-up, discoloured uniforms, and faces and voices of those who had been "through it," and had a good deal more to go through before they would have done with " it "—" it " being the War. Madeleine had seen hundreds such, going up to the line, coming down from the line, sitting round her father's table, taking charge of parties of men, with shy resolution. Little given to guessing, she could have told almost of what they were talking—of what they had done on leave, what sort of " show " they were going to be involved in, possibly of the very inn of the " Lion of Flanders " where they might have snatched a comfortable meal in the intervals of sleeping in their clothes and eating out of their hands. They passed beside her and she smiled involuntarily. Her long vigil had not been in vain. All the English divisions were bound to pass into the Somme offensive sooner or later, and there was nothing wonderful in her meeting two officers whom she had seen before. Nor was it because she was feeling the home-sickness or the loneliness of the acutely sensitive. But just because the starvation of her Fixed Idea had wrought her up to a point culminating at that moment, she smiled.

The shorter, fairer of the two, whose mere name she remembered (for she had that sort of memory, very useful for checking billeting returns), recognized her and spoke to his companion. The other turned. It was Lieutenant Skene, whom she had not seen, or indeed thought of, since the Horse Show. He turned, and their glances met. She saw in a moment that it mattered intensely to both of them what she did, how or why she could not see, but she knew that it mattered. She kept perfectly still, her face moulded in a smile. The door clicked. They were alone. Skene sat before her. What had she done? Nothing. By doing nothing she had placed him there.

He began questioning her: what was she doing in Amiens? and she replied briefly, not thinking of the words. She pushed aside her cup and rested one elbow on the table, her chin in her hand. She stared into his eyes, grey-brown, dilated by shell-fire, and reddened at the rims by gas, but full of feeling which she recognized at a glance as genuine. That feeling was concern for her welfare. She did not admit to herself, still less to him, that there was anything to be concerned about. But it warmed her in the depths of her heart, just as the liqueur he had ordered for her (with sweet cakes, and the way in which he did it showed his solicitude) warmed her stomach. It was true he was talking about himself. She knew in a moment that this was not egotism but English shyness. She answered him in a dream, rocking her body ever so slightly on her chair, as if she were nursing something. Indeed, she was—nursing some part of her spirit, bruised just as violently as her knees had been when the old horse fell down and threw her on to the pavé of the Lille road—for she had just been thrown out of her closed self-control, that

hid unwelcome Truth even from herself, on to
the bare realization of the long fast of two years,
the sharp starvation of two months.

Now he was talking about *her*, with the polite
candour which had made her say, the first time
she saw him, that he was "well brought up"
and "willing." More, he was inquiring about
Georges. She was not surprised; that was all
part of it. She heard herself, as another person,
replying coolly: "He is dead!" and when
pressed further: "He is dead for me." She
could have laughed aloud at the same time, not
for joy, but from the steady mounting beat of her
own heart. His concern was trebled. Her
heart beat faster, not feverishly, steadily. She
had thought of her trouble: "I'll put an end to
this!" She was putting an end to it!

Then he actually touched her, and made sym-
pathetic remarks. He was advising her not to
frequent officers' restaurants, and she replied she
did not care. It was true. She cared for nothing at the moment, had never felt more light-
hearted. He asked what she was going to do
next. She wanted to laugh more than ever as
she said, "Nothing!" He proposed a cinema.
She assented delightedly, feeling as though she
would have proposed it herself in a moment, it
was so inevitable. She made a quick calculation.
Cécile Blanquart and the other girls were at the
office. Aunt Blanquart and the pork butcher's
wife, at whose house she lodged, would not be

shopping in the main streets, rendered expensive by English custom. It was safe enough.

Out in the street she stepped beside him with a pride which, she suddenly realized, she had never known. There are inconveniences about clandestine liaisons. She almost enjoyed the publicity. Fortified by coffee, cakes and brandy, as tall as he was to an inch or so, she seemed to float along on the wings of new-found comfort, effortless, smiling.

The cinema was full. He was nonplussed, she could see, did not know what to do next—knew what he wanted (as she did, and hugged herself), but, being English, had a difficulty in saying it. He wanted her. That was natural enough. She knew herself to be desirable. It amused her to hear him proposing to see her home to her " Aunt's "—for thus she had described her lodging. She let him. It seemed now she had only to go on letting him, and the riddle of life was solved. She had not known an hour before that there was a riddle. Now she only knew she was approaching a solution.

They arrived in the narrow by-street near the cathedral as the clocks chimed four. At that hour the place was deserted. Their footsteps echoed, they might have been treading a world of their own. Madeleine felt it, but noticed that he was feeling something stronger. He had almost shed his English reserve—was talking volubly, about himself—how he had been twice

in hospital, and must now go back to the fighting
—how men like himself wanted a little comfort
before they died. He spoke in English, but she
understood most of the words and all the drift.
His feelings coincided with hers and saved her
the trouble of expressing them, to which she was
unused and averse. At the door of her lodging
they both stopped, she with her key in the lock,
he looking at her with eyes that he immediately
averted, and which pivoted round, in spite of
him, to her. As she turned the key and opened
the door, she said, with the feeling of turning
something in her heart and opening it : " Here
we are ! " Inevitably, as if she had taught him
the words, he was saying : " Don't send me
away, let me stay ! " and with a great sigh of
happiness such as she had felt once before in her
life—another life, surely—she retreated into the
dark entry before him with : " Well then, my
poor friend ! "

*   *   *   *

When Madeleine next had attention to spare
for such matters, the chimes were telling six
o'clock, and through the glass of the skylight-
window a little star twinkled. She became
conscious that he was slowly awakening from the
stupor in which they had plunged each other,
and was lying, open-eyed, waiting for her to
move (just like him). Her mind sprang at once
to the practical :

" What time is your train ? "

" Gone this half-hour ! "

She sat up in alarm : " You will have trouble ! "

" They can't tell to a few hours when I left camp ! "

Reassured, she passed on to the next thing.

" You are hungry ! "

" Yes ! "

She was fully alive to the situation. The pork butcher's wife downstairs had opened, like every one in Amiens who could manage it, an eating-room. The particular public for which it catered were English and French N.C.O.'s of garrison formations, not a field for high profit, but respectable and regular. There was a back room. It was better than courting trouble by going outside. She explained this to Skene as she sat up, shivered slightly at the contact of the air, lit the candle, and tidied herself. She was not ill at ease before him. Thorough in everything, when she gave she knew no stint. She did not boggle over the irregularity of their situation, any more than over her semi-nudity. Why should she ? She had perfect confidence in what she had done, just as in her things, which were clean and good in quality, and in her body, which was firm and fresh with health. Of course, out in the street the conventions constrained one to dissemble, to conceal what one did, and only to show as much of one's skin as fashion allowed for the moment.

But with Skene she was as frank as she had been with herself, poured him out clean water, and explained that with a small gratuity and a generous order, Madame would make no scruple of their having the best time they could. There were the French police to bribe, possibly, and worse still, the English, but it could be managed.

She was proud of Skene when they interviewed Madame. He spoke French with some fluency, and knew just how to flatter the old lady's sensibility and appeal to her greed. When they sat opposite each other in the little back room, he turned on her eyes still bemused, and looked at his watch with frank pleasure : " No train till six-thirty. Still nearly twelve hours ! " he said. Under the table she rubbed his ankle with her slippered foot. Their little dinner ended, as, alas ! all dinners must. The pork butcher's wife, overpaid and adroitly flattered, rallied them, almost blessed them, as, his arm round her waist, her arm round his neck, they mounted slowly the dark, narrow stairs.

Hardly a breath of disillusionment spoiled their few hours together. He took what life could give him—life that was likely to end for him so soon and so abruptly. She, woman-like, put into it something almost sacramental, as though she were devoting to flames some cherished possession, and devoting it willingly. There was nothing Skene could have asked her for that she would not have given him, from money to her heart's blood. He asked simply to be loved—comforted, more exactly, in his starved, war-worn body. That was easy. She gloried in it, even went so far outside her usual self as to point out the bare cleanliness and order of her little room. That was just about the length of her knowledge of English character. A clean room would appeal to him. She never even stopped to wonder that she should be so anxious to please this chance acquaintance—this man of different race, religion, and language. She had never read a novel and was innocent of the romantic theories of love at first sight. She acted as she did from one of her slow-moving, undemonstrative impulses—just then so strong that it amounted to a feeling of almost physical wellbeing in her limbs—traceable, possibly, if she had been the sort to theorize about origins of feeling, to starved maternal instinct. She missed something—petulance, perversity—the whims of a spoiled child that she would have loved to gratify, as she had, long before, in the secrecy of the hut in the Kruysabel. But she did not miss her spoiled child much, for she had instead this good child—this man of quiet good manners, whose behaviour she had noted the first time she saw him, and who now accepted her suggestions without a murmur. So she invited him gently to see how she had moved the few articles of furniture, scrubbed the floor, cleaned the skylight, pasted paper on the damp-stained walls, hung her few dresses on hooks beneath a curtain, and put a rose-coloured paper shade round her candle. She was gratified to see how pleased he was, little suspecting that she had laid her finger on the very deepest desire in him. He had told her that he was no soldier, but a member of a profession that he had practised for twenty years before volunteering in August, 1914. Yet she was very far from forming any conception of the decent orderliness of the life he had left, the life of an assistant diocesan architect in a provincial English town, with its rooted habit of cleanly comfort and moderate happiness, that the war had hurt so horribly ; and she never guessed what dim echoes her own Flemish domestic virtues aroused, of all he had ever felt to be the necessities of existence.

She was even farther away from him when his self-consciousness, awakening with the small hours, drew him to think of the future—of his and of hers. Like many another man in those years, his courage ebbed at the false dawn, and he questioned Fate aloud as to whether he would see another—whether he would ever again know the comfort of her. The simple cunning of her kind led her to propose arrangements to meet him again. This in turn led to the question of where she was to be found. This drew from him anxious questions, that flattered her immensely by the importance he attached to her welfare, but brought back unpleasantly into prominence that other whom she was trying so hard, so unconsciously, to forget. She burst out with a few fierce words, stamping and stamping on that dead image of love to make it disappear from view. It was when she did this, brutally dismissing from memory that spoiled child of her affections, that her new, good, well-behaved child gave her the first taste of his imperfections. He was solicitous, punctilious to a degree, questioned if he ought to take what was Georges'. She would have been angry with him in another moment had not a stronger, surer, more positive instinct prevailed. They had such a little time, might never have another. She wound her bare arms round his head and stifled his questions and doubts against the present reality of her tangible self. And surely she was right. In all those years of loss and waste it occurred to her naturally to build and replace what she could, and all the love and care she could not give to the children she might not bear, she gave to this grown-up child, who needed it, and took it willingly enough, once he ceased to think.

*   *   *   *

In the grey dawn she was up and about, making coffee, heating water for him to shave, helping clean his endless buckles and straps. She let him out in good time for his train, and sweetened her kiss with the eternal hopefulness of that " à bientôt," " until soon," that is the happiest thing

in French farewells.   Then slowly, carefully,
she made herself ready for the day at the office,
proud of the dark touches under her eyes, of the
mat-pallor of her skin, of the little smiles that
curled the corners of her mouth.   And many a
man, seeing her, wished he had been the source of
the deep secret satisfaction she seemed to give
herself that day.

All that week she retained the feeling of having
done a good action—or, as she would have expressed it, had she expressed it at all—driven a
good bargain with Fate.   At the end of the week
" Papa," as the girls in the office called the head
of the room, waited for her and asked her to spend
the Sunday afternoon with him.   It was his birthday, and he and she would celebrate it with a little
Festivity.   She did not look at him for fear she
should laugh, for, taller than he by inches, she
caught the sparkle of the electric light reflected
on the top of his bald head.   She asked, with
averted face, " Will there be many invitations ? "

" But no—you and I alone, naturally ! "

She shook her head slowly from side to side as
she hooked her fur under her chin and surveyed
herself in the little glass that hung on the door
of the girls' lobby.

" But you promised last time that there should
be other times——"   His voice had risen, his
eyes darkened.   It was wonderful what malignity
could still reside in a little old man.   Something
stronger still inhabited Madeleine, since those

123

few hours she had spent with Skene. Once again the blood in her veins had run like molten honey, and she, no spendthrift of herself, had felt in every limb as she gave herself up utterly : " This is right—right—right ! "

She was in no mood for senile trifling, and turned on him with the arrogance of youth, blazing, magnificent : " And now I promise you there will not ! " and left him, breathless and a little afraid.

*　　*　　*　　*

Another week passed. Madeleine became uneasy. The strongest emotional impression will not last. The time she had had with Skeen began to fade into the background. It had been such a minute. It had no result. Instead of feeling perversely resentful against Georges, she now felt so against both of them. Skene neither wrote nor made any sign. He did not even give her the dubious satisfaction of obliterating the shame she felt at Georges' neglect. All this lay, a dumb ache, in her uncritical soul. But she had more immediate cause for annoyance. She became conscious that she was being looked at, whispered about. It did nothing more than ruffle the surface of her self-confidence, but when she and Cécile Blanquart went to the cinema together—she hardly noticed a half-unwillingness on Cécile's part, and that the other girls who often accompanied them had made excuses—she was brought face to face with the matter. Cécile said shyly, in the melodious darkness of the one-franc seats, where one had to keep one's hands in one's lap, because so many soldiers were lonely :

" You know what they are saying about you at the office ? "

" No—what ? "

" Oh—I daren't tell you ! "

Madeleine did not press her. There is only one thing said by girls who cannot mind their own business—having, indeed, no business to mind. Madeleine had never spread nor listened with interest to rumours about other girls, simply because she minded her own business, having always had business to mind. But she knew well enough what the village gossip of Hondebecq was, and had found out that an office in a provincial town is only a village without elbow-room. She pondered a little over the matter, which grew increasingly serious as she did so. She did not bother greatly as to the source of any rumour about her. Spite on the part of " Papa," love of scandal in the heart of the pork butcher's wife of her lodging—mere empty interest on the part of some person or persons who had seen her with Skene or with "Papa," it might be ! The point that disturbed her was the possible effect on her freedom of action. It might make it more difficult for her to profit by the next opportunity of seeing Skene-Georges—for the two were slowly merging into one at the back of her mind. This roused her. She began to think seriously, but in her slow way.

*   *   *   *

Then came a letter from home—from Marie.

She read it several times, by candle-light, lying on her back in her narrow iron bed, one hand holding the pages of British Expeditionary Force canteen block note-paper, which Marie used because it cost nothing, covered with Marie's sloping convent-school writing—the other hand below her head, on which a handkerchief protected the long plaits of her hair, that she had never bobbed at the command of fashion. Gradually she mastered it. Marie was no correspondent ; none of the sort that she belonged to, cultivated letter-writing or exceeded what was strictly necessary. The motive of the letter was baldly stated : " Father demands to know how goes his daughter." There followed a brief résumé of village news. Victor Dequidt was reported missing. Other persons had been married. There had been more bombing near St. Omer. There was no news of brother Marcel ; they feared the worst. Then followed the words : " Father has seen Monsieur le Baron lately. He was furious. It seems that his son Georges has left the French Mission where he was in safety, and has gone to make his training for an aviator in Paris. Madame is desolated " ; and then commonplaces

to the end. " His son Georges " was a way of
speaking Marie had picked up from living in the
Lys valley, in the influence of Lille. It was not
how they spoke in Hondebecq. This displeased
Madeleine an instant. Then the real meaning of
the letter dawned on her. Her father had shown
by his conduct on the day of their visit to the
hospital how thoroughly he understood what was
between Georges and herself. He had made
Marie write—Marie who knew and suspected
nothing. Madeleine—the youngest, the one
who had lived longest with him, who had replaced her mother in the house—responded to the
old man's partiality for her. Unspoken, never
visible, there was a stronger link between them
than existed with the others of the family. She
thought of him with affection. Her mind moved
on. She could see the Baron, stumping up and
down the earth roads, with " Merde ! " and
" Name of a name ! " at every step; and the
dining-room at the château, into which she had
been allowed to peep, when running errands from
the farm. She could hear Placide's nasal chant
announcing dinner : " Madame la Baronne is
served ! " and the Baron, still " Merde "-ing and
" Name of a name "-ing, and the Baronne's tearful
but dignified "Voyons, Charles !" Paris, Georges
was in Paris ! Although affectionate in her way,
she hardly paused to think of her brother Marcel,
giving no sign from his German prison.

*　　　*　　　*　　　*

Then she had one of her intuitions. The very thing. She would teach the gossips of Amiens to tell tales about her—and give them something to tell of, all in one blow. The very economy of the idea appealed to her. There were always vacancies in the big Ministries in Paris, she had heard " Papa " say. " Papa ! " she almost laughed. He would have his Festivity, after all. He should be made to work it. The idea was so new and beautiful that it actually kept her awake for half an hour after she had blown out her candle—a rare thing for a girl of her habits and physique.

The first person who was astonished at the turn of affairs was " Papa." He became aware, as he snuffled with rage and ill-health at his desk behind the screen by the stove, of kind looks and lingerings. His resentment and small suspicions soon melted. He ventured half-apologetic remarks, was not rebuffed. Nor did she hurry away with the other girls, as she had done all the week since his last propositions. Eventually he timidly complained that he had not had his little Festivity, that his birthday had passed unhonoured.

Madeleine felt something, almost compunction, but her Fixed Idea soon resumed its empire over her mind. She listened to him.

On the following Sunday, having drunk her coffee and eaten her roll, she replied to Marie's letter. She expressed her sympathy with all

128

those in the village who had suffered bereavement, sent her congratulations to all those who had bettered their state of life. She asked to hear further of Marcel. She mentioned the Baron and the Baronne in the former category, also the Dequidts. She sent her father much affection and promised to come and see him soon. This was a mere convention. He would have been astonished had she carried it into effect, but it was testimony of her gratitude to him for having guessed her Fixed Idea, and having so astutely helped her. The letter, evidence of an orderly, unimaginative mind, wound up with sisterly affection for Marie—also a convention—for the two girls, realists to the core, knew well enough that they were friendly so long as they remained apart—and kisses for Emilienne. Having completed this, and posted it, she went to second mass at the cathedral. There, when it was over, she sat in the dimness of the sand-bagged windows and the ancient stones. She had never read Mr. Ruskin, never glanced at the moral carvings of the west front, the historical carvings of the ambulatory—sand-bagged as were the first, and removed as were the second now—and would probably have made very little of them, save that they were the sort of carvings one saw in churches. Of all the long romance of that storied pile, from Robert de Luzarches to the German occupation of 1870, she knew and cared nothing—neither for its tons of masonry, glass and wood, nor for the million prayers that drifted on its stagnant air. Nor did she sit there alone from any religious motive. She was not truly religious—too sure of herself, too incurious, she kept of the faith of her fathers nothing but some habits, and some rags of superstition. She left, at one o'clock, when all the English officers were in their messes, and all French homes had that air of preoccupation which accompanies the most important meal of the week. The streets were empty. She passed rapidly to the big shop at which " Papa's " servant was caretaker, and found the side door unlocked. In the back sitting-room Papa was waiting for her, skull-cap, clean collar, eyes watering with pleasure. There, amid solid furniture, marble-topped chiffoniers and chests of drawers, hermetically sealed, chairs and settees upholstered as if for ever, they held " Papa's Festivity." Once again Madeleine was touched when she saw he had ordered red wine to please her. But after the table had been cleared and his senile familiarities began, she hardened her heart. She questioned him straightly and searchingly, making him buy, with information, every liberty she allowed him. She knew well enough how quickly men changed, once they were satisfied, and chose the very moment before he lay back on the plush settee, exhausted by the violence of his emotions, to extract a promise that he would get her transferred to Paris, and a second promise of secrecy—because, she told him, there were so many spiteful tongues. She looked him full in the eyes as she said this, but he was at the stage at which he could only say, "Yes, yes!" intent on gratifying his momentary needs. After this she poured him out some wine, and kissing him on his bald head —for his skull-cap had slipped off—she left him to reflect. She went to an appointment with Cécile Blanquart, whose father was visiting her for the day and chatted to him of village affairs. Her crude psychology was not at fault. For a day or two "Papa" left her alone, but before a week was out he was pestering her again. She took it as a right, believing that men who had once desired her must do so again. In fact, it was this point at which Georges' neglect had so hurt her. But she had made her terms and stuck to them. She reminded "Papa" of his promises, and he demurred, temporized. She cut him severely for two days and brought him to heel. He was not likely to find many women who would have patience with him, feeble and mean about money as he was, in face of the chances of a good time with some English officer. He did as he was told. She had to interview the Controller of the Service, but fortunately Paris was always calling for more and more help to fill the places of men combed out, and she got her transfer, and all the accompanying papers, complete. She was to go the following Sunday. She knew enough of the working of things by now to see

that she was already out of the power of "Papa."
With this, all compunction left her. She promised gaily to dine with him, and he little suspected the real source of her pleasure : the feeling
that at last she would be near Georges, easily able
to meet him face to face as she desired, and that,
once met, she would work on him her charm, in
which she had such implicit trust.

She arranged to meet "Papa" at the station, because, she said, she wanted information about her
train on the morrow. The information she
really required was about that evening's train, the
18.05 for Paris. He drew her into the buffet,
anxious to prime himself for his evening's enjoyment, and she went willingly, careless of appear-
ances now. He ordered two of those compounds
known as Quinine Tonics. She gulped hers
down as the Boulogne-Paris train thundered in,
bent forward to kiss him, and crying, " Au revoir,
mind you are decent to the girls ! " swung out
of the door, across the waiting-hall, and through
the wicket, where he could not follow, as he had
no permit. In fact, he did not try. He was first so
astonished, then so enraged, that he choked over
his drink, and dropped his glass, for the break-
age of which a callous waitress charged him forty
centimes. Alas, that a long career of getting the
most out of women, and giving the least, should
descend to this !

*　　*　　*　　*

"ON LES AURA"

Although so short a time had elapsed, the Madeleine who travelled from Amiens to Paris was a very different girl from the Madeleine who had left Hondebecq three months earlier. The very manner of her shaking off "Papa" showed it. The habit of the village in which she had grown up, regarding railways, consisted in going to the station, hearing when the next train went to the required destination, and waiting for it. To possess and understand a time-table—more, to have mastered the complicated regulations of a militarized station in war-time, was the measure of how far Madeleine had advanced.

She found herself in a Paris that had an air of forced cheerfulness and dumb expectancy. True, the panic of the day of mobilization, growing right up to the Aisne battle, was over ; the alarums of 1918 were not yet in sight. But it was a Paris bereft of men, many a shutter closed ; a Paris as yet unhaunted by Americans, but beginning to be desperate in its pleasures. What its best historians, its great lovers, Murger or Victor Hugo, would have thought of it, cannot be conjectured. Its fabled gaiety was gone for good. Its heroism had that poisoned quality that makes women cover broken hearts with cheap finery.

Madeleine, who had never imagined a town of the size before, spent the first month very quietly taking it all in. She had the sense to see that she must start all over again. She did her work with zest—it suited her. That suited her Controller, who put her to lodge with relatives—retired people of official class, who lived in an "apartment," a tiny flat in a huge block of buildings situated just where the scholarly Pantheon district trails off into the poverty of St. Étienne du Mont. No one could be more self-effacing than Madeleine when she wished to. During her first weeks in Paris she attended to her work, lived quietly with Monsieur and Madame Petit, dressed soberly, glanced at no one in the street, or in the great office where her duties lay. She made herself amiable and useful in the small precise household, left it in time to catch her 'bus, that landed her opposite the bridge, across which towered the world-famous gallery in which the Ministry to which she was attached was housed. She made herself agreeable to the girls with whom she worked. Some were country girls, shy or inefficient, but there was not a Fleming amongst them, and she concealed her opinion that she knew better than they about most things. As for the native Parisiennes, of whom all sorts and conditions were gathered into that great harbour of steady work and sure pay, she admired their ferocious femininity and put up with their moods —even when they called her " Boche du Nord " —the equivalent of calling a Worcestershire girl a Welshwoman—which they did at times, out of sheer dislike of her demure capacity. To have seen her, no one would have suspected that

134

she was gleaning every scrap of information she could with regard to the Flying Corps units that formed the Air defence of Paris. And she had better opportunity now. Paris was by no means the town-just-behind-the-line that Madeleine was used to. Information was to be had, people got to know things and talked of them. Her Ministry, engaged in rationing one of the necessities of life, rationed Flying Corps troops among other people. She missed nothing. At last she found what she was looking for.

*   *   *   *

In one of those innumerable lists of men that were being produced by Government Departments all over the world, as well as in her particular Ministry, she saw the name Georges d'Archeville. It was a list of those young men designated, with the picturesque appropriateness of the French language, as "aspiring aviators" who were "directed towards the Front," that is, being sent into the line of battle. Madeleine and another girl were crossing them off the lists of the garrison of Paris. She stared so long and heavily that her companion bent over her : "What ! You can't find it—but there it is ! "

Madeleine ticked the beloved name and went on, as in a stupor. This was really a blow. To come to Paris had seemed to her, somehow, the satisfactory culmination of her long vigil. She felt sure she would be successful in finding him.

She had found him indeed. What now ! The
Paris garrison was not concerned with the fate of
" aspiring aviators " once they were struck off its
rolls. Their fate was not indeed in much doubt,
but there remained the horrible uncertainty as to
which of the graveyards behind the four hundred
miles of Front would hold his grave. At this
point her common-sense and practical knowledge
of affairs deserted her. She just wanted him,
that was all. Feigning a headache, she excused
herself and got leave to go home ; but instead of
going, she lingered about the quays and bridges,
never lovelier than in winter twilight, with golden
wraiths of leaves spinning in the bitter wind along
the severe, well-proportioned grey lines of
masonry. The fresh air calmed her ; hunger at
length drove her back to the Petits' apartment.
She did not notice at first anything in the manner
of her hosts. The only thing that she noticed
was that M. Petit, as he handed her a letter,
used the phrase :

" It came about four o'clock ! "

That was the hour at which her eye had caught
the name in the fatal list. All the threads and
tatters of superstition that clung to her Flemish
soul took life and substance at this. She muttered the words, " Ah, yes ! I expected it. It is a
word from home ! " She passed, quiet and self-
possessed, to her little bedroom, one of those
little rooms which lead one to ask if they were
intended by the architect for anything, or whether

they might not be an inadvertence. Lighting her candle, she sat on the thin coverlet of her bed, that reached from the tall window to the door, and resting her feet on the lower shelf of the wash-stand, thrust her thumb into the envelope and burst it open. It was from Skene. It was what is called in those English romances Madeleine had never read or imagined, a "love letter." It asked her to spend his week's leave with him. That much she saw, and then put it down and buried her face in her hands. She had expected it to contain news of the death of Georges. Why or how she thought anyone should write to her on such a subject is one of those mysteries that hang about the most clear-minded, least bemused of people. She had felt it rather than thought it, and the revulsion was for the moment too much for her. She was roused by the clatter of plates, and the acrid voice of Madame Petit, keeping the supper within the smallest possible bounds. She changed her blouse, washed and did her hair, and hurried out to help Madame.

During a meal whose frugality would have driven a monk from his vows, she heard M. Petit say, " Well, have you good news from home ! " and herself replying : " Yes. My brother writes to say he has leave, and asks me to go home to see him ! "

She afterwards reflected that she could not have invented a better answer. The envelope was stamped with the British military postmark.

The old man was inquisitive, and there was no
knowing what use he might not make of any conclusion he drew. To have a brother in the English area was the one feasible explanation.

* * * *

These considerations did not weigh heavily
with her, however. She slipped away as soon as
she could, and read her letter through again and
then again. There was much in it that she did
not come within a long way of understanding—
descriptions of the life of decent civilized men in
camp and billet, not to mention trench and dugout. These simply conveyed nothing and did not
interest her. Then there was an involved scrupu-
lousness that she had no means of sharing. But
the main motive that had caused the writing of
those four sheets was clear enough—Skene really
wanted her. And if she did not admit it to herself, she wanted to be wanted. She did not reply
to the letter, but put it away in a safe place, a
little lock-up box in which she kept her immediate
savings and a trinket or two, and went to her
work in the morning, a changed woman. She
had regained in a breath her old sureness. She
now saw herself again the woman she desired to
be. " If I can only see him face to face " still
ran in her mind, but this time it was Skene whom
she hoped to see. Insensibly the symbol had
changed, the emotions remained. She thought
the matter over in her cautious way. He had

supposed her still to be in Amiens and had written there. By good luck she had sent a card (one of those war postcards, all khaki and azure and sentiment) to Cécile Blanquart, having it in her mind that Cécile would describe to the full, in her next letter home (for Cécile was the sort that wrote once a week), anything that she, Madeleine, did. It had been an act of petty pride. It now seemed like the work of Providence—Cécile had redirected the letter, and here it was. Madeleine did not mistake what it meant. He wanted a week, like the few hours he had had, in Amiens. That was natural enough ; she saw nothing in it. In her experience men were like that, and she secretly approved. For a week, at least, she would have some one belonging to her ; beyond that she did not look.

After twenty-four hours' consideration she took the letter from its hiding-place, replied to it in most measured terms—judging to a nicety, by some instinct, what would make him say a little more and say it a little plainer, without committing her in any way. A week passed, and back came a further letter. It filled her with a sort of steady glow. There was no mistaking it. He had written for a room in an hotel he knew of at the other end of the city, on the steep hill that leads from behind the big stations to Montmartre. She did not reply until old M. Petit, looking at her over his spectacles, asked her : " Well, and your brother ? "

She gathered herself together mentally. Of course, she had to fend off all that sort of thing. She replied briefly : " I am going home for a week ! "

That evening she sent Skene a card on which Union Jack and Tricolour were entwined. She wrote with a sort of exultation : " I wish to be all yours." Such an outburst must have been caused by something deeper than the paltry bickering of a little old man, or the prospect of meeting a young one with whom she had once passed a few hours of intimacy under the stress of strong emotion.

*   *   *   *

The day came. She got her week's leave. It is one of the victories of women's entry into ordinary commercial activities of business houses and Government offices, that they have forced some humanity and reason into the mechanical discipline of such places. Having made no plans, she had put her few belongings into one of those black hold-alls that make all French travellers seem countrified, and stood on the platform of the Gare du Nord, waiting. She had dressed herself carefully—more carefully than usual, with hardly a spot of colour, and was conscious that every inch of her that was covered showed the finest possible value for the money. Her hands, neck and face had lost nothing of their firmness and pallor. The figure she cut seemed to culminate in the little leather satchel clasped against her fur—as if she were holding her heart in reserve, and defending it at the same time. The train roared into the station, and after a moment's confusion, she saw Skene coming towards her. She had been wondering fearfully for a moment if he would come, if she would recognize him, if any unforeseen obstacle would arise. When he reached her, she turned up her face and gave him her rare smile. When he slid his hand under her arm and hurried her down the platform to catch one of the few taxis, she pressed ever so little against him. Never in her life had she been happier than in hearing those heavy boots clanking beside her. Now that he had come she knew she was right. Skene was neither exceptionally handsome, brave nor rich—and she would have thought nothing the more of him if he had been. She neither knew nor cared for heroes of fiction, but admired the clean, athletic type of young man just then beginning to be popularized by the cinema. Skene had the looks and bearing of what he was—an average Englishman of the professional classes, who had passed through the successive stages of discomfort, danger, all but death. He had the sure movements, straight glance, and agreeable carelessness begotten of this, grafted on to middle-class standards of manners. Superficially, at any rate, he was more considerate than his nearest French equivalent would have been.

All this, which would have disappointed or amused many a Frenchwoman, captivated Madeleine, and in the taxi she gave up her lips to him with rich joy at the unmistakable warmth of his feelings. The moment, however, the taxi stopped at the restaurant she had indicated, she made herself prim and aloof. She had not wasted her time since she had been in Paris, and knew her way about. The restaurant dated from the period of those great Exhibitions that had served to rehabilitate Paris after 1870. Originally the home of the sort of people who gave some shadowy substance to Murger's bohemian Paris, it had long become the classic rendezvous of English and American visitors and of Frenchman who wanted to sacrifice style to price. It still had the red-plush benches and gaily frescoed walls of romance, but the service and cooking were what Frenchmen call "serious." The place had just been worth preserving on a commercial basis in the commercial era, and consequently had been preserved.

Madeleine had lost nothing of her idea of celebrating an occasion. She ate heartily and did not refuse to drink with Skene. He was, of course, ravenous, and in the state in which drink had no effect on him. She smiled demurely across the table at him, more at home every moment. He was also amused at something. He had only known Paris fifteen years earlier, as a young architect half-way through his A.R.I.B.A., and was marvelling at the change—at the figure she cut in those surroundings that had for him such different associations : she almost bourgeois —he in the fancy dress of his uniform. Her manner with the waiter was perfect, and perfect her assumption of respectability. He loved it, felt almost at home, too. For in their secret hearts both of them were domesticated, conventional to the core. Both of them loathed the War and all it had brought. It was the queerest of contradictions that forced them to comfort their ultra-respectable aspirations in such a place and such a manner, both spoken of even in war-time, by many people, as " irregular."

*　　*　　*　　*

The meal at an end, they went, as a matter of course, to a cinema. One did, in war-time. Skene, who at home would hardly have walked to the end of the street with such an object—Madeleine, who had hardly heard of such a thing before she went to Amiens—went to the nearest cinema because it was war-time and no one wanted to think. Walking in the brisk air of a Parisian winter evening, good meat and drink within them, they enjoyed themselves prodigiously, Skene because he had existed in dubious snatches of comfort for a long time, and was likely to so exist for an indefinite period—Madeleine because of the reality of a man at her side. He was making jokes about the Place Clichy being the Place

Cliché ! She did not understand in the least, but laughed because he was happy beside her. And so on to the gaping portico of one of those establishments which advertise what is known in France as " spectacle de famille." This last was being loudly cried by a person, paid to do so, at the door—who added in stentorian tones that soldiers went in free, and nursemaids half-price. It was typical of Skene that he paid for two of the most expensive seats, and placed Madeleine in the one that gave him the best view of her profile. The film, unfortunately, was a French one, not an American. That is to say, instead of being confronted with the improbable adventures of a man looking somewhat like Skene, Madeleine realized with a start that she was watching a love story in which the principal character was a tolerable travesty of Georges d'Archeville, and behaved with just his perverse petulance. She turned her head, smiled at Skene, played with her programme, smoothed her gloves, and arranged herself with minute care for her costume and the possible effect of the seat on it. It was no good. Cinema screens are insistent. It is difficult to avoid that great glare of white, with its intriguing figures in motion. It revealed to her what she would never have invented for herself—the idea that, like the hero of the film, Georges neglected her because he was engrossed by some other woman. She could not dismiss the idea ; did not try, perhaps. She felt suddenly more wounded

than she had ever felt since August, 1914. That
Georges might be hurt at her sharing an English
officer's week of Leave never occurred to her.
To her practical soul, with its incapacity for
flights of imagination, things seemed all too
readily what they appeared to the eye. Suddenly she rose.

"This representation is rasant," she said to
Skene, and marvelled a moment, as they threaded
their way out, at his docile good temper. Not a
grumble, not a protest. He just followed her
and snapped up a taxi. In it he was more
solicitous than ever, gentle, kind, with a Mid-
Victorian kindness she had never known—the
manners of one whose boyhood has been un-
spoiled by bitter thoughts about money.

They reached the little hotel at which they had
dropped their baggage, and he handed her in.
By this time his way with her was having the
queerest effect. Had he been thoughtless, bru-
tal, she would easily have braced herself to meet
it. As it was, she felt something slowly dissolving
in her. She held herself in yet a little, approving
the place he had chosen, clean and reasonable in
price. But when the door of their little room was
bolted, and she stood in front of the mirror by the
rose-coloured curtains, unpinning her hat, he
came gently behind her and slipped his hands
under her arms. It was just Georges' way.
She burst into tears. The moment the first sob
had shaken itself free—for she did nothing by

halves, and when, rarely, she cried, she cried bitterly—she knew she would feel better. Skene let her droop on to the bed and sat beside her, one arm round her, making very small comforting remarks in French and English alternately, but no inquiries. She kept her handkerchief tight pressed upon her eyes with both hands, but her sobs were lessening, and with every moment the agonizing vision of Georges with some one else grew smaller and fainter. She leaned ever so gently against Skene, who tended her as a woman might a child, did every little service for her, amazing her, who had never been so treated since she was four years old. Gradually she slipped down into the comfort of those hard hands, whose fingers kept something of the skill and discrimination of such as have been used for wise, gentle occupations. But only when she was at ease, with dry bright eyes and braided hair, did he seem to think of himself, and then only to ask so humbly for what he wanted. She gave him all herself, fiercely, as if for ever to prevent any of her from escaping again into those other hands that had neglected her so. More, when they two swam slowly back to the surface of normal existence again, in the quiet of the night only broken by the discreet bubbling of the calorifère in the corner, she told him the stark truth of herself and Georges, with a bareness of exposure of her very soul she had never before permitted, of which, perhaps, she had never before been capable. And when at last they slept, in each other's arms, it was the deep sleep of emotional reaction, for no less than she, Skene had looked for years past on utter shipwreck—obliteration of his individuality in the dark mud of Flemish trenches —and knew from a different point of view all she suffered, and what comfort she clutched at.

*   *   *   *

The next day passed in that atmosphere known to English honeymooners. Not a trace remained of the emotions of the evening before—nothing but two healthy young people out for a holiday, both in the most incurious state of mind, and easily amused. The things they missed seeing far out-numbered those they noticed, as is the case with honeymooners.

Madeleine was so used to the English that she hardly smiled when he turned the little hotel upside down in order to have a hot bath and an egg for breakfast. The establishment, at length conceding these recondite advantages, ceased to interest them. They went out into the busy streets, in the frosty air, Skene's hands in the pockets of his " British warm," Madeleine with one hand tucked into his arm, the other holding her fur tippet closed across her throat, as she saw other girls doing. To Skene, a free morning in Paris could only, by habit and association, mean one thing :—pictures. To Madeleine it could only mean another :—shops. As they descended

into the roaring heart of the city, never busier
than in mid-war, they found some of the galleries
were still open, and Skene took her from room to
room, pointing out old favourites, lamenting new
gaps left by careful storage of some of the more
valuable masterpieces. She moved beside him,
confused, uncertain whether to blush or look away
in front of many a splendid nudity, but drawn
by the spirit that was on both, to squeeze his arm
a little. In the mood of the moment she unconsciously identified herself with all feminine beauty,
and he acquiesced. But he was not less in holiday mind than she, stood patiently for half an
hour at a time in big shops, watching her wringing
out to the uttermost centime the best value from
scowling shop-girls. Skene begged to give her
what she wanted—he had managed to visit three
field cashiers and get francs from each—he had
a pocket full of money. She accepted, loyally
keeping herself within limits and wasting nothing.
Both of them had their shocks. In one of the
turnings off the rue de Rivoli they met a tall fresh-
cheeked young man, scented and glittering, in a
grey-green uniform Skene identified as Russian.
Skene fell into a growling condemnation of all
" Base Pups," " Head-quarter people," etc., etc.,
incomprehensible to her, save its long-stored
ill-humour. But she was after all only saying the
same thing in French, when a frail, fair, over-
arranged lady kept her waiting in the glove
department of the Bon Marché, when Skene

heard her grind her white teeth, with : "That
sort of animal doesn't know what time's worth ! "

*　　*　　*　　*

The next day was still queerer. Skene wanted
what he called " a day in the country." Madeleine had no idea what he might mean, her notions
of a holiday being confined to Church Festivals.
She went with him, however, down the Seine
Valley, as far as the regulations permitted. She
gathered he once had regular haunts here, had
gone by steamer with companions. She taunted
him laughingly with having been one to " rigo-
ler " in his youth. She began to suspect that he
was much richer than his worn khaki and careful
trench habits made apparent. He took her to a
well-known beauty spot, all shuttered and sad
with war and winter, roused the proprietor and
persuaded him to give them food and drink in the
mournfulness of the dismantled salle à manger.
The proprietor, like so many others, had lost an
only son. It took a lot of gentleness and some
of Skene's Expeditionary Force canteen cigarettes
to thaw him. But gradually he expanded into
the graveyard interest of his kind. What were
the trenches like ? Were the dead buried properly ? Would one find their graves ? Skene
told all he could, painted a true picture as far as
he could, exaggerating no horror, slurring over
none of the stark facts. The old man was appeased. He liked to know. So his son was

149

lying like that, was he, amid the Meuse hillocks !

Madeleine took no part in the conversation, but sat looking at Skene, totally uninterested in what he was saying, enjoying the masculinity of his movements and gestures. She was beginning to be curious about the one thing that ever aroused her speculation. What was this man's position in life ? The men talked on into the winter dusk, the " patron " offering liqueurs and cigars. She and Skene missed their train back and had to walk to a neighbouring depôt, and get seats on an army lorry. Skene tipped the driver and Madeleine saw the man's face. That night, as they lay side by side in the sober companionship that both of them felt so right and justifiable, she asked him of his home. She was somewhat astonished at the result. He talked for twenty minutes, and was all the time incomprehensible to her. The old house in the Cathedral Close, the hereditary sinecure descending in the one family—the semi-public school, wholly leisured-class prejudices and scruples—the circle of maiden aunts living on railway dividends—the pet animals—the social functions—made her pucker her smooth, regular forehead with complete mystification. She could make nothing of it except that every one in England was rolling in money.

*　　*　　*　　*

Another day followed, and another. The end of the week was at hand. As it approached, they

both regarded the impending separation calmly.
The emotions that had brought them together
were of the sort that will not keep. Neither of
them were bohemians of the true water. The
life of the little hotel where they slept and the
restaurants where they fed was soon drained of its
attractiveness. If Skene really wanted anything,
it was to be back at his job in England. If Madeleine ever asked herself what she found lacking in
those brief days, the answer would have been a
farm of her own, a settled place in some village
community, and, perhaps, children. But she did
not ask herself such questions, nor did Skene
admit for a moment that there was anything to
desire other than what they shared. But there
fell long silences between them. The tittle-tattle
about topical events interested neither of them.
The little news they could tell each other was told.
They could not talk of Georges. Their only
common memories were of the farm and the
Easter Horse Show of the division. Both sub-
jects were stale. The small attempt Madeleine
made to understand Skene had led her into per-
plexity. Skene had let her more intimate self
alone, having neat provincial notions of chivalry.
The excursions of peace-time Paris no longer
existed. The cinema and most theatres bored
Skene. Madeleine could not sit out concerts.
The day before the last, they went at Skene's
suggestion to the Sorbonne. He wanted to feast
his eyes, that must so soon look at decauville rail-

ways and trench-mortar ammunition, on the Fresco, by Puvis de Chavannes, which decorates the lecture hall of that institution.

He had first seen it as a young man, and the impression it had made was undimmed. He loved that blue-green twilight in which statuesque people stood in attitudes among Greek pillars and poplar trees. He loved it with an English love of things as they are not. Madeleine gazed at the great lecture hall. At last she said, " It is not then a church ! " No fool, she had grasped the speculative, investigating atmosphere.

" No," Skene replied, " it is a higher grade school ! "

"As school decoration, it is not ver' useful ! " Skene had nothing to say.

Later, as Skene wished to dawdle over some architectural drawings in the Cluny Museum, she said frankly she would look at the shops. Their time was drawing to a close. The next day was the last. Skene did not know how to say that he hoped to meet her again. Did he ?

*   *   *   *

For Madeleine it was easier. She simply went on behaving beautifully. The week had not been spoiled by one cross word. To the end, she found no fault with Skene, herself, or Fate. Such tenderness as life had not already rubbed out of her, showed itself in her solicitude as to his sandwiches and half-bottle of wine. It would

be cold, she warned him, as they paced the platform of the Gare du Nord. If he passed by the
farm he would say a word to her father and Marie.
He promised, stoical as she, and habituated to
War-time farewells. He did not allude to the
future. She kept herself wrapped in uncritical
passivity. The train was made up. She saw
his out-of-shape cap, khaki back, and tightly
clothed legs disappear successively in the doorway of the carriage. He came out again, having
secured his corner, and they paced the asphalt of
the station for yet a few minutes, in silence.
Then at shoutings and whistlings and blowings
of tin trumpets, without which no French train
can start, he disappeared again, but, the door
closed, hung out of the window. The train was
full of French leave-men, many drunk. One in
particular, who was wearing a bowler hat on his
uniform, noticed Skene and Madeleine just as
the train began to move, and shouted, " I know
what you've been doing, English officer and little
lady ! " Skene waved and was gone. Madeleine turned and went. "Know what you've
been doing " rang in her ears. A smile curled
the corners of her mouth. Men looked after her
again now that she was alone. She walked,
taking pleasure in exercise and the keen air, to
the little hotel in the stony street, paid the bill,
with the money Skene had given her, reclaimed
her hold-all, strained to bursting with the things
he had bought for her. Then she demanded a

taxi, which she dismissed in front of the Pantheon,
and walked on foot to Monsieur and Madame
Petit's.   She ascended the stone stairs, cold and
bare as penury, and knocked.

Monsieur opened to her with a short piece of
candle, carefully screened in his hand.   He
closed the door and led her into the fireless dining-
room, from which her room opened.   He peered
at her.

"Well, this war, how goes it?"

"But gently!" she replied, not guessing what
he was driving at.

"Come, your brother told you nothing?"

In a moment it came back to her, that she had
been spending a week's "leave" with her "brother."   She faced the peering old eyes.

"You know that the men in the trenches never
say anything!"

He was rebuffed, but tried again.

"The Boulogne train must have been very
late!"

But she was on her guard now, and replied
readily enough :

"Very late.   The Bosche were bombing
Amiens!"

The old man grunted and left her.   In her
own room she smiled at her reflection in the glass.
She was looking magnificent, feeling magnificent.
To come from at least some degree of luxury, if
not from home and love, at least from entertain-
ment and admiration, to the bleak realities of her

daily life, did not daunt her Flemish heart. She unpacked and undressed methodically, passed her hands over that flesh that had been so generously caressed, and seemed rounded and fortified by it, and wrapped herself in the hard-worn bedclothes, warming them with her vitality. Could Skene, buttoned up in his "British warm," miles away on the northern railway, have seen her, he might have been attracted, he would not have been harrowed or flattered. She had rubbed off the contact with him by the passage of her hands over herself. She rubbed him off her soul no less easily. She was at her place in the Ministry on the morrow, and save that her appearance of well-being excited desire or envy, created no sensation.

Then as the days passed, very slowly, and all the more surely, reaction began to set it. She did not analyse it or express it, but it was there. The old feeling of having been done, cheated ! There was the old void—and Skene, against whom she bore no malice—she was partial to him, rather —had tried to fill it and failed. It was not in him. Too well behaved, too incomprehensible, too English, he had, in fact, not asked enough of her. She would have felt more at home with him had he been subject to those moods of feverish desire and cold disgust that she associated with all that was most admirable in men. For that male perversity by which, when it existed in her father and the Baron, in "Papa," and Monsieur Blanquart,

in fact in all men, was the very thing by which war
had been brought about, and caused her separation from Georges—when it appeared in that
Georges himself, became simply one of his attributes. Her "good child" bored her. Her
spoiled, imperious one was what she needed.

*   *   *   *

The evenings lengthened. February came,
and the Bosche retreat. Marie wrote that she
was trying to get back to Laventie, where things
were in a pitiable state, but good land must not
be allowed to lie waste. They despaired of Marcel. Madeleine did not reply to this letter.
The farm and all it contained seemed very remote.
Yet the letter was a comfort; it brought no bad
news, and no news was good. Already, she
thought again of nothing but Georges. As for
any practical plan to find him, she had long come
to the end of the expedients that her not very
strong imagination could devise. She just
wanted, and waited.

The chief of her department in the Ministry
was one of those politicians who found the War
dull. Its concentration upon the one great effort
to beat the Bosche, and preserve the French
nation alive, robbed such a politician of his living.
There was little scope for anything but messing
with contracts, trying and necessarily unspec-
tacular. This one among the party-bosses of the
French Chamber hit upon a plan which would

advertise him, and at the same time give a sort of rallying-cry and style for the next political stunt. He saw shrewdly enough that Peace would one day burst upon an astonished world, and that those who were unprepared for it would be badly left. And what would be the best starting-place in the new Peace atmosphere ? Why, obviously, to be hailed in a million farms, a million small shops, as " That brave Monsieur Dantrigues— he was good to our poor boys in the hospitals during the War ! " It could be used as common ground for the Action Française on the one hand, and the extreme socialists on the other. And no one dared raise hand or word against it. The quickest, cheapest and best way to set it afoot was, of course, to make use of the organizing power of his immense department, the ocean of needy vanity in which the hundreds of temporary typists and girl war-clerks swam ; the comic papers could be got to blaze it about—they were invariably hard up.

So it was that Madeleine, in common with all her companions, found herself invited to take part in a gigantic Charitable Fête. They were given little cards with the particulars—certain elements of costume were to be uniform, also an electric lamp in the hair, and a basket of gifts. They were to meet in the Tuileries, at certain spots indicated by numbers, from which decorated lorries would take them to the various hospitals of the metropolitan area, to distribute an Easter gift to every sick or wounded soldier. Monsieur Dantrigues was smart enough to see that this was much more effective than the same thing carried out near the Front. For if a man has incurred a gumboil guarding a railway in the Seine Valley, he likes just as well to be treated as a "brave wounded," and is just as likely to vote subsequently for the man who organized people to think him so. On the other hand, the real fighting soldiers, nearer the Front, would mostly be killed and never vote at all.

The idea caught on. Generals, clerics, ladies old and young, blessed it and gave funds for costumes and presents.

* * * *

Never did government department function so ill as that which contained Madeleine, as the ten thousand charitable maidens prepared themselves for the fray. Madeleine entered into the affair rather than make herself conspicuous. She had no sentiment about other people's soldiers, no anxiety to please men who did not interest her. But she went, took her number, arranged herself with sense and taste, and found a little comfort from looking nice. She managed to get a double supply of gifts and send one lot to her brother Marcel, hoping that it might bring a sign from him in his German prison.

The day came. Released at an early hour, the girls dispersed to costume themselves. The

short-sleeved tunic of thin white material, with
its girdle of artificial ivy leaves, suited Madeleine.
Even Monsieur and Madame Petit, never prodigal of praise, admitted that she looked well.
When she arrived at the rendezvous, she created
some sensation. The uniform dress brought out
precisely her better proportions and carriage, all
her good looks that depended on health and hard
work. As the lorries that were to take them to
their places swung alongside the pavement, one
of the girls said of her, " That great Flanders mare
ought to have two seats allowed her ! " but the
very spite in the speech was a compliment to
Madeleine. They were set down on the steps of
one of those great palaces of stone, common in
Paris, that had been aroused from centuries of
slumber by the War, and now sheltered hundreds
of narrow white beds. Among these, up and
down great vistas of ward and corridor, the girls
processed, music in front, bearers of lighted
candles behind. The fête, designed by a lady
of cosmopolitan education, just then very intimate
with Dantrigues, had elements of English carol-
singing and German Christmas-tree effect, mixed
with French delight in spectacle and uniform.
Then the girls were divided into pairs, and given
so many beds each for the distribution of gifts.

   Madeleine was frankly bored with the whole
thing. She hardly bothered to make herself
agreeable to the men in her section of beds—
passing them with a word or two of conventional

good wishes, holding her clean, fair-skinned, smiling, slightly obtuse profile high above them, stepping easily, unencumbered by the basket on her hip. At the end of her bit were several empty beds, the nursing sister on duty explaining that the occupants were more or less convalescent, and had leave. She did not trouble to hurry off elsewhere, nor to obtain a fresh supply of gifts. The more or less innocent flirtations, which the other girls saw as one of the chief attractions of the business, did not excite her. The electric globe in her hair, which annoyed her, went out, and seeing a glass door leading on to a verandah, all dark and quiet, she slipped through unseen. She had hardly drawn the door to behind her than she had a peculiar sensation. She had stepped into a mild, humid spring night, the stars of which shone above the garden plantation of the place, beyond the stone pillars of the balcony on which she stood. But in her own mind she had stepped through the separation of over two years, as one puts one's foot through a paper screen. Georges was near her, she knew. The back of the balcony, against the glazed windows of the ward, was lined with a kind of fixed garden seat used by the convalescent. One of these convalescents was seated, lying there rather, his attitude expressive more of exasperation than of physical weakness. Before she could analyse or act upon her queer feeling of nearness of Georges, his voice arose from that recumbent figure, in

the quakerish simplicity of French intimacy :
" It is thou ! " was all he said.

She flung down her basket and sunk on the
seat beside him. Galvanized into sudden life,
he heaved himself up, clutched her in his arms,
bent down her face to his. For some time, who
can tell how long, neither of them thought of
anything, content just to feel the emotions of the
moment. Amid these arose the jangle of a bell.
It brought Madeleine to her senses at once. It
was the arranged signal—five minutes' warning
before the charitable maidens rejoined their
lorries. M. Dantrigues' lady friend had thought-
fully suggested that some of the young women
might want to put themselves tidy. Madeleine
stood up, telling Georges briefly what was intended. He replied with an army word, intimat-
ing how much he cared. She was tender, docile,
careful with him, spoiling him every minute.

" Yes, yes, my little one. I know. But it
is worth more to arrange where we can meet.
Your Mado will wait for you wherever you
say ! "

It was the pet name he had for her those ages
ago in the Kruysabel. At the sound of it, spoken
as she spoke, all that lost Peace-time ease arose
ghostly before them. He vented his indignation
against Fate by picking up her basket and flinging
it into the night, where it crashed softly among
earth and leaves. The gesture delighted her.
It was the old Georges, the real " young master "

161   M

of first love. She had been terribly frightened by his first greeting, that meek " It is thou ! " so unlike him, that he had uttered. He pleased her still more when he went on :

" If that's your bell, you'd better go. Don't get caught in this sacred box, whatever you do ! "

" Tell me where," she whispered.

" I'll find a place and let you know. I must get out of here. If not, I'll burst myself as I have bursted so many Bosches. Where do you live ? "

She told him, pressed a kiss on his lips, and was gone in a flash, quiet, confident, alert. She was herself again.

The journey back to the rendezvous in the lorry was noisy and amusing. A score or two of young women, mainly at the minx stage of un-attachment, chattered and squabbled, mimicked and raved. Madeleine sat in a corner unheeding. From the rendezvous home she took no account of time, nor place, could not have said by which street she passed, or at what hour she sat down to the Petits' supper. They were rather nicer than usual to her that night, feeling perhaps that she was a credit to them—for the charitable fête had been discussed from every possible point of view in that quarter of shabby gentility, and every one in the block of flats knew that the Petits' lodger had taken part. Madame Petit had seen to that. But Madeleine was not responsive—

162

wrapped herself in a brown study—or was it a
golden dream?—and retired early to her room.

* * * *

The next day she was the same—quiet, polite,
but detached, went to the office as usual, returned
at the same hour, replied to questions in mono-
syllables, went to bed early. Monsieur Petit
began to have his suspicions—could it be that
the young woman had fallen in love ("made a
friend" was the expression he used to his wife)
at the fête?

The next morning, as they sipped coffee in
their several déshabillés, there came a knock on
the door. A message! Monsieur Petit, who
took it in, handed it to Madeleine through the
two inches that she opened her door. He dressed
hurriedly, agog with excitement. The hour at
which she usually left for the office passed, and
she did not appear. Finally, she did leave her
room, at nearly ten o'clock, dressed in her best,
carrying her holdall and a hat-box.

"Good-bye," she said. "I have left everything
in order and the week's money on the dressing-
table."

Monsieur Petit stammered, "But why?"

Madeleine's eyes gleamed in such a way that
he stood aside to let her pass. "Because I
am leaving," she said. "Make my adieux to
Madame. She is occupied, I know!"

And the old man stamped with rage as he heard

her firm footfall descending the stone stairs. She was going, taking away a secret with her. Almost as well have taken one of the bronze figures of saints or knights on horseback from the dining-room—that would have been no more a robbery than to take away a secret from that little home where bronze statuettes and curiosity about other people's affairs were the only luxuries.

At the foot of the stairs Madeleine hailed a taxi and gave an address in the north-western quarter of the city, from the paper in her hand. Then she folded the paper carefully, and replaced it in her hand-bag with her money and little mirror, as the vehicle bounded down the Boulevard St. Michel. Poor Monsieur Petit was not to be allowed to forget her departure. Three days later the postman brought a letter for Madeleine. Monsieur Petit turned it over and over, his fingers itched. Then something in his memory of super-annuated government service stirred. He knew what it was, and told his wife, nodding and glaring malignantly.

" I have sent hundreds in my time. It is the dismissal ! "

It appeased him somewhat, for naturally he could imagine nothing more fatal than to be dismissed from the service of the government he had served for fifty years, and which paid him his pension in consequence. Retribution indeed had fallen on Madeleine, in Monsieur Petit's eyes.

*　　*　　*　　*

"ON LES AURA"

Could Monsieur Petit have divined whither
Madeleine had flown, could he have followed
her, confronted her as he longed to, crying, " See,
abandoned girl, cheater of my curiosity, how Fate
has overtaken you ! " it is doubtful if Madeleine
would have bothered even to laugh at him. She
sat perfectly upright, swaying with the rocking
vehicle, staring at the chauffeur's back, as she
was carried down steep crowded streets, across
wide vistas of bridge and quay, square and avenue,
up into quiet, almost sinister-quiet, respectable
streets. Dismissing and paying her taxi, and
watching him out of sight, she shouldered her
baggage and found her way along by sign and
number to a tall block of small flats, like a hundred
other such. She waited a moment, hesitating
between dislike of the concierge and equal dislike
of becoming conspicuous by standing in the road.
Finally, she walked boldly in, disregarding the
gaping eyes and mouth that followed her from
the basement, mounted to the floor she required,
and knocked. She had to repeat her knock
more than once before it was answered and the
door was left unlocked for her to push open.
There was no one in the little vestibule. She
dropped her things, and, guided by Georges'
voice, found the bedroom, where Georges, who
had pulled the clothes over him again, was cursing
the cold floor he had had to tread. That was the
real Georges, the man who wanted her without
bothering to get up to open the door for her, the

165

man for whom she would have died. She put her arms round his neck, and bent down to him, so that he could have her.

*　　*　　*　　*

He was very much real Georges that day. He lay in bed until hunger forced him to rise, and then would neither dress nor shave. He was not of that type that lives on the interest of the past, nor hurriedly discounts the future. Nor can it be said that the thought of Lieutenant Skene crossed Madeleine's mind. Had it done so, she might have reflected how much more she loved this, her spoiled child, than that, her good one. But she, too, was absorbed in the present. She did not even remember the Ministry, whose service she had so peremptorily abandoned.

When the first gladness of reunion was slowing down into the assurance that she really had got him back, and had now only to devise how to keep him—a task she did not feel very difficult—she began to question him, very gently and indirectly, as to his plans. She remonstrated with him on the folly of their being there together, an object of interest to the concierge, still more on his insistence that she should stay there. But he only shouted that he would " burst up " all the concierges, and she had to humour him and promise to stay for the present at least. Not that he threatened to leave her, but that she would not and could not threaten to leave him. At length,

in the evening, as he sat in gown and slippers
before the fire she had made, at the supper she had
fetched and set, while she tidied the room strewn
with his things, he began to think of her, asked
for her father. He only asked one or two brief
questions, not being the man to take deep interest
in anything outside his own comfort. When
she had answered, he just said : " This sacred
war ! " Nothing else. But Madeleine knew
what he meant. There it was, all round and over
them, enveloping, threatening, thwarting. No
less than he, she rebelled against it, in her decorous woman's way. But for him she rebelled
against it twice over, hated it, made it responsible
for his loss of health that was new, and his violence
that was habitual—forgave him, on account of it,
his carelessness of her—this way in which he
wanted to live—the obvious fact that he had had
other women in this room. She did not reflect
upon her own record, then. But she coaxed him
to take supper—she had bought the war-products
that were nearest to the hare-paté and spicebread
and confiture of old times—gave him a bowl of
hot wine and water, as she had many a time that
he had found her, he, glowing and triumphant,
with a dog at his heels. And sure enough, under
the spell of her magic, in that firelit bed-sitting
room of the little flat in Paris, there came back,
gradually but surely, the Georges of old days.
His worn cheeks filled out, his eyes were less
sunken, his hand less thin and shaky. He began

to hold up his head and hum a tune. She hung near him, watching him, foreseeing not only every need, but every whim. He became almost liberal, expansive. He had fourteen days' " convalo "—a visit every day to the hospital, which institution would not otherwise bother about him. At the end of that time he would either go back to hospital, or up to the front. He did not care which, he said, smiling. For the first time since she had rediscovered him, he did not call anything sacred, wish to "burst" anyone, or use the expressive, untranslatable verb " foutre." She cleared away and tidied up and prepared herself for the night, as he sat glancing through the newspapers humming to himself, content, asking nothing. When he felt tired, he just turned out the light, and rolled into the place she had made warm for him.

*　　*　　*　　*

Days so spent soon pass, nor is there anything more tragic than physical satiety, with its wiping out of what has gone before. Madeleine, not naturally apprehensive, would have gone on had not hard facts pulled her up. Georges had spent his pocket-money on paying the quarter's rent of their retreat. She had spent hers on food for him and herself. No bohemian, she began to take counsel with herself as to how to obtain fresh supplies. One source of funds she dismissed at once. She would not ask Georges for a penny.

That would have seemed outrageous to her. She did not attempt it. She had a handsome sum in the Savings Bank at Hazebrouck. But how get it? She did not want to write to Monsieur Blanquart or to Marie. Even if they could have withdrawn it for her (and the difficulties of such a step she did not clearly foresee), they would both of them have found out sooner or later something about Georges. And that she would not have for all the world. Her father she could trust, but she also knew his ingrained habits regarding money, his incapacity for reading and writing. A letter would simply stupefy him. If he got some one to read it to him, he would simply be stupefied the more. His Madeleine spending her savings? Never! He would do nothing. Should she, then, go by train and get the money? There would be endless difficulties in getting authority to journey into the British Military Zone—but the great difficulty to her mind, the insurmountable one, was to leave Georges for two days. She was nonplussed.

Just then it happened that Georges, turning towards her in one of his more expansive moments, said, in his spoiled way: "My God, how I want you!"

Occupied fully with him at the moment, her mind retained the words, her memory searching for the last occasion on which she had heard them. Georges went out to his club that morning, leaving her sewing, washing, doing a hundred and

one jobs in her thorough housekeeper's way.
She sat brooding, almost waiting for some stroke
of luck to help her with her difficulty. Suddenly
she remembered who it was that last used that
phrase—Lieutenant Skene. She sat down at
once and wrote to him. She had no scruples.
All the English were rich. This one had no out-
let for his money. She had been worth it. The
reply came in three days, to the post-office address
she had given. It brought a hundred francs.
They lasted a week, and few people could have
made them last more, save that Georges only came
in to supper now. He was getting restless, smelled
of drink. She wrote again to Skene. No reply
came. Instead there came the end of the fortnight of Georges' "convalo." That day she
sat alone waiting for two things, a letter bringing
money, or Georges bringing fatal news. Either
he was not well enough to go back to the front,
so that his state must indeed be serious, or he was
well enough, which was even worse. She dared
not ask him ; he vouchsafed nothing, seemed well
enough, but restless. She, meanwhile, for the
first time in her life was feeling really ill. She
had never met before with this particular cruelty
of Fate, resented it, but only felt worse. Perhaps
the town life had sapped her vitality. Perhaps
Georges had brought home from his hospital,
on his clothes, in his breath, the germ of some
war fever. The following day Georges was
excited, and talked loud and long when he came

back from the club. Her head felt so strange she did not understand.

*   *   *   *

Perhaps it was as well she did not. Georges had been granted another fortnight's "convalo," but it was not that. It was the news of the battle of Vimy that excited him. The English, of whom he was good-humouredly jealous, had taken that battered ridge, disputed for years. There was talk of eleven thousand prisoners and a quantity of guns. He had missed being " in it." But with the news came rumour more important still. The French were preparing a great offensive in Champagne. He would not miss that one, sacred name, not he ! The spirit of that period of the war, the spirit of " On Les Aura " burned in his veins like fire. As he strode and shouted about the room, cursing his " convalo " that, a week ago was all he desired, because now it prevented his being in the show.

Madeleine had the queerest feeling of all her life up to that day, for she was not a girl to faint —a sinking feeling, not painful, rather comforting. Then nothing. Then a reawakening, not so comfortable, dismay, weakness. Georges, who did nothing by halves, became, for the nonce, generous to the utmost limit of the nature of a man born with a silver spoon in his mouth and a cheque-book in the pocket of his first suit. Probably it never crossed his mind that she had taken infection from some carelessness of his. But he did better. He promptly called a young doctor of his set, who, having been badly wounded, was now permanently attached to the Paris garrison. Between affection for Georges and a handsome bribe—for the proceeding was thoroughly irregular—flat contrary to every by-law of the town and every order of the Medical Service—this young man took Madeleine in hand, visited her daily, did what was necessary in the way of prescribing, got a discreet sister of charity to nurse her. Being a man of the world, he further suggested to her, as soon as she was well enough to make inquiries, that she would not care for Georges to see her in her present state. That kept her quiet during the weeks of recovery. But there came a fine June day when she was well enough to walk out a little in a Paris ever more feverish and deserted. Then the young doctor, as thorough as Georges or herself, told her the truth. Georges' thoroughness had taken the form of borrowing the identity disc and pay-book of a hospital casualty whom he resembled in height and complexion. The young doctor had connived at the fraud, with the cynicism of Georges himself and all his set. Thus furnished, Georges had gone straight into the heart of that ghastly failure of the French in Champagne, during May, 1917. The hurried scrutiny of his credentials had not found him out, he was in the line and fighting when his half-recovered health broke down once more, and fatally. He was buried in a huge, ever-growing cemetery, near the Aerodrome, at Avenant-le-Petit.

*   *   *   *

When Madeleine realized it, she sat still, looking at nothing, gathering within her all her physical vitality to meet this blow to the spirit. On her face, refined by illness, was something of the look that horses have under heavy shell-fire, bewildered resistance to the unknown. The young doctor let her alone for twenty-four hours, and then very gently led her mind back to practical considerations. The period for which Georges had hired the flat was expiring shortly. Had she money, or the means of getting some ? It did not take her long to run over the alternatives —an attempt to get back into some sort of office —or a begging letter to Skene ? She avoided both, not from any sense of shame, but simply because now Paris and its life had no meaning for her. She had wanted Georges. She had said, " If I could only see him ! " She had seen him. Now she would never see him again. Why bother ?

The young doctor then suggested that he could obtain her a permission to travel by train to Haze-brouck. This brought to her mind the almost certain death of her brother, Marcel, in his German prison camp, and of Marie's return to Laventie. The mere name of the market town

called up at once associations so potent, so much
more real than all that had happened since. The
farm understaffed, the old father being swindled
out of billeting money ! Those were realities.
Those things appealed to her more than this
tragic dream-life. She accepted gladly the young
doctor's offer, and left him looking after her and
muttering : " What a type, all the same ! "
But she had no special contempt or dislike for
him.

She left Paris in the same way as she left him.
The old sacred towers, the new garish restaurants,
the keen bitter energy, the feminine grace, of that
metropolis of the world, that had once again had
the enemy at its gates, and was yet to be bombarded by such engines as had never before been
turned upon city of man—she turned her back
upon it all, and, for her, it was not. On a grey
July day she entered the train. As she travelled
homewards, the day grew greyer and wetter.
She passed, unheeding, through an immense
bustle between Abbeville and Calais, and down
to St. Omer. Her train stopped frequently, and
she glanced, uninterested, at the trains and trucks,
materials and men, that choked rail and road.
About her, people talked of the great offensive
the English had begun, from Ypres to the sea.
She looked at the crops and houses, thought of
her father, whose very double, tall, old, dark-
clothed, and bent, she saw in almost every teem-
ing field of flax or hops, grain or roots, of that

rich valley. Perhaps she had occasional bitter spasms of anger against this war, that had enslaved, and then destroyed Georges. But to her, facts were facts, and she did not deny them.

*   *   *   *

Outside Hazebrouck the train stopped interminably. The guns had been audible, loud and angry for some time, but the long roll of them was punctuated now by a sharper nearer sound, that clubbed one about the ears at regular intervals—artillery practising, no doubt, she thought. After waiting in the motionless train as long as she considered reasonable, she got out, finding a perverse satisfaction in the use of her limbs, swinging down the steep side of the second-class carriage of the Nord Railway, and asking for her box and " cardboard " (containing hats) to be handed down to her. Shouldering these, she marched along the asphalt with which the prodigal English had reinforced the embankment, showing no concern at the cries of " They bombard ! " shouted to her by her fellow-passengers. She passed the engine, from which the driver and fireman were peering ahead. The fields were very deserted, but she was hardly the sort to be frightened in daylight, or dark either. She passed the points where the Dunkirk line joined that from St. Omer. Near by, stood a row of cottages, known as the " Seven Chimneys," the first houses of Hazebrouck, on the station side.

Her idea was to leave her trunk at the estaminet, for her father to fetch in the morning. To her astonishment, the whole row appeared deserted, empty, doors open, fires burning, food cooking. Somewhat nonplussed, she stopped a moment to get her breath, pushed her box behind the counter of the estaminet, where she was known, and then passed on, with her "cardboard," keeping the path that separates the St. Omer road from the railway. Where this reached its highest point, just at the entry to the town, she happened to glance across the rich, lonely, hedgeless fields towards the Aire road, and saw, on that side, every wall and alley black with people. She had no time to reflect on this peculiarity before she was deafened by such a roaring upheaval of earth as she had certainly never imagined. It took away her breath, wrenched her "cardboard" out of her hands. For some seconds she could hear nothing, see nothing, but when her senses returned, the first thing she noticed was the patter of falling debris. The shell had fallen in the ditch of the railway embankment, and made a hole the size of the midden at home, and three times as deep. She picked herself up from her knees, dusted herself, recaptured her "cardboard," and passed on, greeted by a long "Ah—a—ah !" from scores of throats of the spectators, a quarter of a mile away. The incident annoyed her. They were bombarding, and no mistake. But it would take worse than that to prevent her from crossing the railway under the arch, and taking the Calais road. The rue de St. Omer was empty, but undamaged. They were a jumpy lot, she thought; it revolted her to see all those good houses, left unlocked and open to all the ills that attack abandoned property. There was not even another shell-hole nearer than the station, so far as she could see. She would have liked a cup of coffee and a slice of bread, but the town was empty as an eggshell. She heard another explosion behind her as she reached the Calais pavé. The persistence of those Bosches ! But she was persistent too, and gathered her damp clothes and battered " cardboard " to her, as she strode vigorously home. She was not sentimental—no one less so, but it may well have been that her blood quickened, and her rooted strength returned, as she found herself, once more, facing that salt wind, under those low grey skies, among which she had been bred and born.

At length she came to the earth road, the sign-post, and the turning, and saw the farm, the fringe of dead wallflower stalks on the ridge of the thatch, the old " shot " tower by the bridge over the moat. It was between six and seven when she passed the brick-pillared gate, noted a new bomb-hole, and signs of military occupation. Entering by the door, she found her father in the passage.

" It's our Madeleine," he said quietly.

Madeleine kissed him and told him to fetch

her box in the morning, from "Seven Chimneys."

He said, "Thy room is empty," and went into the kitchen, while she said a word to Berthe. It was true, her little room was just as she had left it a year before. She noted the fact with quiet satisfaction, but did not bother over the significance of it—over the fact that her father, who usually paid so little heed to anything that went on in the house, had kept her room untouched and empty for her. She quietly accepted the fact, conscious that he felt that neither the God to whom he muttered prayers on Sunday, nor the various temporal powers whom he obeyed, when he had to, on weekdays, really understood him or cared for him as his younger daughter did. She sat down with him, in the dim kitchen, to the evening meal, by the light of the day that was dying in thin drizzle and incessant mutter of guns. Once some fearful counter-barrage made the old panes of the oriel window rattle, and the old man said :

" It's a swine of a war, all the same ! "

Madeleine replied : " It's something new for them to be bombarded in Hazebrouck ! "

" I'm going to take the money out of the Savings Bank," he commented. In his mind, unused to the facilities of book-keeping, and cradled in the cult of the worsted stocking for savings, he probably thought of his money as being held in notes or coin in the stoutly-barred vault behind the Mairie. After a long pause, during which he surveyed her hands, busy with household mending, somewhat neglected since Marie had relinquished it to Berthe, he spoke again :

"You are quite a fine lady of the town !"

"That will soon pass," she answered, without ceasing to ply her needle.

Later he said : "You know Marie has returned to Laventie ?"

Madeleine nodded. The remark was not so stupid as it sounded. He knew she knew the fact. It was his way of appealing to her.

"Now you have come back, you will be just the Madeleine you used to be, and all will go on as before, won't it ?"

Her nod was all the answer he asked.

Once again he spoke : "You know Marcel is dead ?"

Again she nodded. Again it was only his way of saying, "Come what may, you will see me through, we shall not be worse off for the cruelties of Fate !" She understood and acquiesced. Nothing else passed until with "Good night, father," and "Good night, my girl," they parted.

Of her life during the past twelve months and all it had contained, not a word.

PART III
LA GALETTE

PART III

La Galette

THE late summer of 1917, the summer of Haig's offensive from Ypres, was one of the wettest of the war, but the days following Madeleine's return opened fine.

She was up betimes, and soon made herself apparent in the life of the farm. Harvest must begin the moment things were dry enough, and before they became too dry, so that the cut grain would neither sprout as it lay, nor spill itself as it fell. Besides herself and her father, they had Berthe, and the family of Belgian refugees, two boys too young for service, and eight women of all ages. A thoughtful government had added two Territorial soldiers of the very oldest class, who could easily be spared from such military duty as they were fit for ; and to this, a still more thoughtful Madeleine mentally added some amount of help that could be extracted, by one means or another, from English troops resting in the area. At the moment of her return there were no troops, but artillery came on the following day. There also came a platelayers' family from Hazebrouck, whose house was too near the big shells that had fallen. Madeleine drove a hard bargain with them, work in the fields as the price of a loft in the outhouses, until the latter should be required for potatoes. But these matters were not her first concern. She made a long and careful scrutiny of the billeting money that had been paid during her absence. Marie was too accustomed to the rough methods of those who live on the edge of the trenches, and knew little of the fine art of making the English pay.

Madeleine went to see Monsieur Blanquart in the morning recess of the school, and found him perceptibly greyer and more harassed, almost snowed under by the immense weight of paper, by which a government, in sore straits, discharged its expedients upon its humbler representatives. In addition to the correspondence and registration necessitated by general mobilization, and by the occupation of an allied army, there were now circulars and returns concerning food production, waste prevention, aircraft precautions, counter-espionage, and the surveillance of prices. In such circumstances, Blanquart probably wished her back in Paris, but she insisted. After bitter argument, he suddenly surveyed her with a gleam of interest.

"There, you aren't greatly changed ; but what induced you to leave a good job in the Ministry ? "

Madeleine realized that she was an object of admiring interest, with who-knows-what history invented for her by Cécile. She pushed it all aside. " I had better things to do than to go mouldy in an office. Now, Monsieur Blanquart, for the month of March, there is only seventy-five

francs marked down. How do you explain it ? "
and so on.

*   *   *   *

She came back from the village across the
fields, scrutinizing the crops, the workers, the
new drains and telegraph wires the English were
putting in everywhere. Already, in a few hours,
her short assumption of town life and habit was
dropping from her. She had put it away with
the town hats Skene and Georges had bought for
her, in the " cardboard," on the half-tester of her
bed. She went bareheaded, already stepping
longer and holding her skirt, with both hands,
up from the wetness of the knee-high root crops,
and away from the waist-high grains. Her
illness had squared and filled out her figure,
deprived it of its virginal severity, and now the
refinement that indoor life, suffering, and im-
paired health had given to her features and skin,
was yielding before fresh air, good food, vigorous
action, and the habit of command. Only her
straight glance, and erect carriage, that she had
taken to town remained as the town was forgotten. The town could not take those from
her, the country could only confirm them. Two
officers' servants, who had let the chargers they
were leading graze surreptitiously on the rich
second cut of the water-meadows by the little
stream that issued from the moat, hastily pulled
up the horses' heads, and resumed the road. She

had made herself known to the new unit that morning, already.

In the dark passage she ran into a dragoon-like figure, that even her accustomed eyes mistook for the moment for that of a soldier. Then she saw who it was, swallowed a lump in the throat, and said :

"Hold, it is you, Placide, enter then, and be seated ! "

"Ah, it is you, Madeleine, returned. How do you go on ? "

"But well ! and you ? You can surely take a cup of coffee ! "

"I shall not say no ! One wants something to give courage in these times that are passing ! "

Madeleine was busy over the coffee-pot, and only said : "Monsieur the Baron and Madame the Baronne have had a sad loss ! "

Placide sighed like an eight-day clock running down, and then began. It took ten minutes for her to give her description of the reception of the news of Georges' death at the château—of Monsieur's fit of crying and swearing—of Madame's fainting and prayers. Madeleine stood before her, hands on hips, planted, resisting the sudden, unexpected agony of reviving grief. When Placide remembered what she had come for (eggs and anthracite) and had gone, accompanied by a Belgian with a barrow, Madeleine poured her untasted coffee carefully back into the pot, and slipped out by the back door and away over the fields.

In a few minutes she was mounting the steep sodden path to the Kruysabel. The sun was coming out, and all around the earth steamed. The hunting shelter, intact and not noticeably weathered, had yet an air of neglect. Grass grew where grass should not, the windows were dim with cobweb and fly-smut. The door stuck, and inside the air was warm and mouldy. The photos stared at her, the guardian spirit of the place, as she moved from room to room, tried handles, dusted, rubbed, and shook things. The seats invited her, the mirrors showed her active restlessness. At last she stood still, and some spasm of acute realization seemed to gather and descend on her, and she wrung her hands. " What will become of it all ? " she cried aloud. It, undefined, being the old happy easy life of pre-war. A great sob broke from her, and at its sound in that lonely place of memories, she pulled herself together, put away her things, and looked up. As she trod the reeking moss and gluey mud on the way home, she seemed to be treading something down into the earth, as, alas, many another was to do, like her, throwing in vain a little mould of forgetfulness on the face of recollection that, buried, yet refused to die.

*   *   *   *

Day succeeded day, mostly wet, almost always

noisy. The interminable offensive dragged to its sodden end. Unit succeeded unit, and then French succeeded English, and even the heroes of Verdun, Champagne, the Argonne had no good word to say of their new sector. Gas they knew, and shells and machine-gun fire, but to be Drowned was the last refinement of a war that had already surpassed all notions of possible evil, all tales of Sedan, all histories of old-time carnage.

All this made little or no impression upon Madeleine. The old life had slipped back upon her like a glove. German bombs dropped in or about the pasture, spoiled her sleep, made her apprehensive of fire and damage. Otherwise she merely learned from the talk around the kitchen stove that the war was just what she had always felt it to be—a crowning imbecility of insupportable grown-up children. All that one wanted was to be left tranquil. There was always plenty to do, and, if one were only left alone, money to be made. Economics, politics, sociology were beyond her, and had they not been so, they would have weighed with her no more than they ever have done with agricultural, self-contained, home-keeping three-quarters of France. That Germany was anxious for her young industries, England for her old ones, France for her language and racial existence, that governments grow naturally corrupt as milk gets sour, by mere effluxion of time, that captains of industry must be ruthless or perish, all this did not sway

her mind.   All one wanted was to be left tranquil.
Tranquillity being denied, she did the best she
could.

The officers who hired the front rooms, the
men and animals billeted in the farm buildings,
the N.C.O.'s, orderlies, what-not, might be
dispirited, jumpy, no longer the easy-going
confident English of other years, but they still
bought what she had to sell, and paid for what
they had—more rather than less, as the con-
scripted civilian, craving the comforts from which
he had been torn, replaced the regular soldier or
early volunteer, who had never known or had dis-
dained them.   She got a good deal of help with
the harvest.   The English had all sorts of stores,
appliances, above all, plenty of willing arms, that
she wanted.   The troops " in rest " were glad
enough for the most part, when off duty, to do
any small job to take their minds off the world-
wide calamity that enveloped them, or that gave
the momentary illusion of peace-time ease and
freedom.   Owing to the submarine campaign
they were rather encouraged than otherwise.
The harvest, though not magnificent, was fair,
and the ever-rising scale of officially fixed prices
left always a larger margin of profit.   Thus
" One does what one can ! " was Madeleine's
appropriate comment, when asked.   Very little
escaped her, as that murderous sodden autumn
closed in.

*   *   *   *

It was about Christmas time that the bombardment of all the back areas, especially Hazebrouck, recommenced in earnest. It was the period at which the Germans regained the initiative. Madeleine noticed a fact like that. She noticed also the extraordinary thinning out of the troops. They either went forward into the line or far back, into rest, beyond St. Omer. But the headlines of the papers, the rumours her father brought home from the estaminet, moved her not one whit. The Russian revolution, the advent of America, the British and French manpower questions, Roumanian or Syrian affairs, all left her cold. She read of them in French and English impartially, with all the distrust of her sort for the printed word. It was not until she heard the Baron descant upon the situation, during a visit he paid her father, that she began to take any serious account of the way the war was trending. The Baron had been severely shaken by the death of his son. A view of life, which seldom went beyond personal comfort, had been vitally disconcerted by the final dispersal of one of its cherished comforts, the idea of a son to succeed to and prolong the enjoyment of life. He had the gloomiest forebodings, blamed Russians, Roumanians, English, Americans, Portuguese, Turks, Germans, in turn for the dark days certainly ahead. Madeleine listened with the tolerant submission proper from a chief tenant's daughter toward the master. When

the Baron spoke of " my son," her just appreciation was never misled into thinking that he meant
her lover. The two were distinct. She had
her own bitter memories, black moods, tears
even. That was her affair. The Baron's loss of
his son was his, a different matter. She sympathized demurely. As for the news he brought,
the probable German offensive in the spring, she
made a rapid calculation, and dismissed the
matter. Not good at imagining, she could not
conceive of anything the Germans might do that
she would not outwit. The crops and animals,
she reckoned, could be stored in safety, the money
and valuables she could trust herself to take care
of ; the solid old house and furniture she could
not picture as suffering much damage. Of any
personal fear for herself she felt no qualm. Except for a few moments during her illness in Paris,
she had known no physical terror since, an infant,
she had ceased to be afraid of the dark, finding
by experience that it did not touch her. She
poured out the Baron's drink at her father's re-
quest, and let him talk.

Poor Baron, though Madeleine did not realize
it, what else could he do ? Born so that he was
four years too young to take part in the war of
1870, he was now eight years too old to take part
in that of 1914. He could only fight with his
tongue, and that he did. But he was fundament-
ally unchanged, rallied Madeleine on the havoc
her good looks must have wrought in Amiens and

Paris. Madeleine smiled dutifully. To her he represented one of the guarantees of order and stability. Without an elaborate argument, she concluded that so long as there was a baron above her, and her father, there would be, at the other end of the social scale, labourers, refugees, all sorts of humble folk just as far beneath the level at which she and hers swam. It seemed just that those above and those below should be equally exploitable by the adroit farmer's daughter, anchored securely midway.

*   *   *   *

Spring came, the spring of 1918 : surely the most tragically beautiful of all the springs the old world has seen ! The frosts and darkness passed. Flowers came out in the Kruysabel. It was a busy time of mucking, ploughing, rolling, sowing. Nothing happened. Hazebrouck, too much bombarded, ceased to hold its market. Madeleine went to Cassel instead. The news of the great German break-through on the Somme did not even impress her, she was busy preparing to get the main-crop potatoes in, before Easter. Let them fight on the Somme, so she might sow Flanders.

But three weeks later there did occur at length something to impress her. On the unforgettable 11th of April, 1918, the guns were very loud. On the 12th there were hurried movements of troops. All sorts of odd rumours came floating back from all points between Ypres and La Bassée. The Germans had broken through ! The Germans had not broken through, but had been thrown back ! Estaires was on fire ! Locre was taken, and so on. Madeleine had occasion to go to the Mairie, to argue as to why her old Territorials should have been recalled from the farm, and found Monsieur Blanquart packing all his records into a great wooden case. He stopped and stared at her :

" What are you doing, Monsieur Blanquart ? "

He raised his hands with unaccustomed nervousness.

" It is a formal order from the Government ! "

He would not listen to her tale of billeting money unpaid, and government fertilizer not delivered : " There are other things to do at this moment," was all he would say. For once Madeleine did not get her way. That impressed her. The next day the horizon to the south and east was black with pillars of smoke. By night these became pillars of flame, biblical, ominous. The incessant sounds of battle changed in timbre. The heavy bombardment ceased. Nearer and nearer crept the rattle of machine guns. Madeleine had one or two errands, and returning by the village shortly afterwards, was astonished to find all the shops shut. Vanhove, the butcher, was loading his best brass bedstead and mattress on to—what of all conceivable vehicles ? Madeleine stared before she took it in. It was the roller, the road roller. None other. The well-known road roller the English had installed. Built by Aveling & Porter at Rochester in the 'eighties, it had ground and panted its unwieldy frame northward through many a township and village of England, passing from hand to ever poorer hand, as it deteriorated, until finally the obscure and almost penniless Rural District Council of Marsham and Little Uttersfield, failing to sell it, had painted their name on its boiler and kept it. Unloaded, like so many other derelicts, into the arms of the British Expeditionary Force in the glad enthusiasm of 1915, it had served the turn of an intelligent English Engineer, who, early in the war, had discovered that roads and railways, food and patience alone could win in such a struggle. He had soon been shipped off to the East, lest he bring shame upon his betters, but his roller had remained for years now, on that section of the Joint Road Control of the Second English Army, with the French Ponts et Chaussées Authority, who divided acrimoniously between them the control of the Hazebrouck sub-area. The machine had become a portent in Hondebecq. The children had swung behind it, horses ceased to shy at it, and Madeleine herself had come, in time, to have something almost like affection for it, as a monument of the queer, wayward genius of the English. No such rollers ever rolled the roads of France, but Madeleine had found it useful for both rolling and traction. She had made friends with the two middle-aged, sooty-khakied Derbyshire men who lived with it and got them to do jobs for her. Now, she laid a hand gingerly on the warm shining rail of the " cab " and asked of the driver.

" What are you doing ! "

" Got to go, mamzelle, partee, you know ! "

" You like a ride, miss ? Get up and we'll take you as far as St. Omer ! " his mate added. " Alleman's coming, you know ! "

Something fierce prompted Madeleine to say : " I'm not going to run away ! " But Vanhove, having hoisted his bedstead into the tender, was persuading the men to drive on.

Madeleine saw the lever put over, and the ponderous machine of another generation roar away upon the cobbles, its single cylinder panting desperately. Then she felt indeed disturbed, as though she had been forced to part with a conviction.

*　　*　　*　　*

As she went back to the farm through the fairy beauty of the evening—(were ever evenings so beautiful as those of the April retreat ?)—her step was no less firm, her glance as calm as usual. Passing over the plank bridge, and entering the house by the back, she was confronted by the spectacle of Berthe in her best hat, with a bundle.

" I'm going ! " said the apparition simply.

" What has come over you ? "

" After you were gone, an English wagon
came, all full of people from Armentières way.
The secretary of Nieppe told the patron that the
Bosche are in Laventie, and that Marie has left,
so the Patron has taken the tumbril and gone after
her potatoes ! "

Madeleine was at no loss. She even approved
the old man's determination. Only she considered that it would have been better for her to
go.

" You stay here," she said.   " I'm going up to
the château to borrow the young Baron's
bicycle ! " She knew well enough that Georges'
machine was stowed away in the coachhouse.
On that she could catch her father, and send
him back. But she had not reckoned up the
situation.

" No," said Berthe, " I'm going ! "

" Why, you're not frightened like that silly
lot from Armentières ? "

But the terror-stricken faces and bandaged
heads of those civilians in the lorry, who had so
narrowly escaped the battle, had broken Berthe's
nerve—which was never the equal of Madeleine's.
She shouldered her bundle.

" I'm going ! " she said simply.

Madeleine was not accustomed to being dis-
obeyed, and there is no knowing what she might
not have done had she not been in a hurry herself.

" Very well, go then ! Tell the Picquart

family to lock up the sheds. I'm going after the patron !"

" The Picquarts are gone, this half-hour, with their things in the wheelbarrow !"

Just then the breeze that stirs at dusk swung open the door, and there entered into the darkening passage with startling nearness the rat-tat-tat-tat-tat of German machine guns. Madeleine flung away : " Go and burst yourselves as quick as possible, heap of dirtiness !" she cried, and set off at a run for the château.

The village seemed even more ominous than before, now it was half dark, and not a light in the abandoned houses. Some English transport was crossing the square, however, with the patient sour look of men going " into it " again—" it," the battle. She turned into the steep silent alley that led through the iron grille, to the " drive " of the château, and broke into a run again on the smooth gravel. She had not gone twenty yards before she jumped as if shot. A black figure had risen behind the trunk of a tree with a sharp " Hish !" She fell sideways, clutching an elm sapling that bent with her, staring. The figure made two steps towards her, and she, petrified, could only maintain her balance and stare. Then with infinite relief she heard : " Tiens, it's you, Madeleine ! What do you want ? "

" Why, Monsieur le Baron, I didn't know you !"

" Be quiet then. There is some one wandering round the château. It may be the Bosche ! "

" What, are they here ? "

" The village has been formally evacuated.
One expects them from one moment to another ! "

At that instant steps and voices could be heard
on the terrace surrounding the house, which, on
account of the winding of the drive by way of the
old moat, was just above the level of their eyes.
The Baron, quivering all over, not with fear, but
with sporting instinct, brought his spiked camp
stool to the charge, and tiptoed noiselessly up the
bank. Madeleine, clutching her skirt with one
hand, swinging herself up by the undergrowth
with the other, arrived beside him just in time
to see two familiar Australian figures looming
leisurely in the darkness. In another instant the
Baron would have sprung, with no one knows
what results. Madeleine pushed past him,
stepped over the flower-bed that bordered the
terrace, and walked up to the visitors, addressing
them in their own inimitable language, learned
from their own lips in the kitchen of the Spanish
Farm :

" Hello, Digger, what you want ? "

The tall lean men turned without surprise :
" To get in," replied the nearer.

Madeleine hastily translated. The Baron,
after staring a moment, led the way to the back.

The château possessed, of course, no bell or
knocker, as Leon, the concierge, or his wife, were

always to be found near the gate, to steer front-door visitors round to their appropriate entrance, and open for them. Lesser mortals came to the kitchen door, where Placide dealt with them as St. Peter is reported to deal with ambitious souls in another place. Since the war, and more especially since the concierge and all his family had been evacuated, the whole of the windows and doors were closed, bolted and shuttered.

The first object that met the gaze of the little party, as they rounded the corner of the building, was Leon's garden ladder, reared against the window of the Baron's dressing-room, in the eastern wing, from which protruded the hind-quarters and legs of a man, in stout service riding breeches and dirty boots.

"Thunder of God," cried the Baron, seizing the ladder and shaking it violently, "come down, or I'll bring you!"

An Australian added quietly, "You'd best come down, Mercadet, and tell Jim!"

A few hurried calls in Franco-English and laconic Australian replies, and a French inter-preter climbed, an Australian soldier slid, down the ladder.

"Well, sir," demanded the Baron of the former, "you have large views of your duties!"

"Sir," replied the interpreter, "the place is officially evacuated. We have a right here. You have not!"

"I have said I will not budge," replied the

Baron, folding his arms, " and budge I will not ! "

" Monsieur le Baron," interposed· Madeleine, " all these will be very useful if the Bosche come ! "

The Baron strode to the heavy kitchen door and struck a succession of blows with his stick, shouting at the top of his voice, " Placide, open then, you are as lazy as stupid ! "

Very shortly a light glimmered and the bolts shot back. The door turned, and Placide barred the way, as an old-fashioned clothes-horse covers a blazing fire. It took her a moment or two to understand.

" Ah, it is you, Monsieur le Baron ! "

" Did you think it was the devil ? "

" I was upstairs seeing to the calorifère of Madame, who is in the chapel. I thought you were gone to the village ! "

Her master pushed past. " Here are officers come to billet. Are the rooms ready ? "

He had, of course, assumed that none but officers would dream of coming to the château of Hondebecq.

Madeleine, by the light of Placide's candle, soon knew better. The Australian who had spoken was a Colonel, the other two and the French interpreter were privates. As they trooped into the passage, the Colonel called over his shoulder, " Come on, boys ! "

From the kitchen garden, where they had sat silent and unnoticed spectators of the scene, there emerged a Lewis-gun section and orderlies.

Beyond them transport was dimly visible : mules silent as their drivers, standing as if cut in stone.

"Madeleine," called the Baron, "explain to these gentlemen that all my servants have run off, but that Placide will serve supper as soon as may be ! "

The Colonel, however, was busy with his machine gunners. The "cubby hutch," as he called Leon's potting shed, half-way up the drive would do for one position well, but he wished to command the garden and meadow beyond, and the fields skirting the village on that side. Madeleine understood perfectly. "There is the cellar skylight, level with the ground."

The Colonel went to look. "It fits like the tail of Barnes' donkey ! " was his only comment.

Before he would sit down to his meal he asked : "Do I get the old man right, that his wife is here still ? "

"She is praying for her son in the chapel ! "

"Is he wounded ? "

"He is dead."

"He'll be just as happy if she keeps alive. I've got a limber going back St. Omer way. She'd better go in that ! Tell 'em ! "

Madeleine explained the offer to the Baron, who thanked the Colonel profusely, saying that it was worthy of one gentleman to another.

The Colonel not understanding, when his mouth was empty, bowed as one unaccustomed and inquired : " It is his wife, isn't it, all correct ? "

Madeleine confirmed that the Baroness was " all correct."

But the Baroness was an obstacle. First Placide, then the Baron himself went up to see her. She would only moan : " No, let them kill me, I shall see him again all the sooner. Besides, it is too late, and I am at least warm with the calorifère ! "

Then Madeleine went up. There was nothing dramatic in the meeting between those two, the mother and the mistress of a dead man. Madeleine said steadily : " Madame, Monsieur Georges would prefer you to go ! "

" You think so ? "

" I am sure, madame ! "

" In that case, I will ! "

Madeleine helped her. But no one, unless it was the French interpreter, realized the pathos of the moment. The limber had been furnished with cushions, a small trunk, and a wooden box of Placide's. The driver had announced that he was " going by the dirt roads, it's easier for wimmen." Then that faded lady kissed the man whom she had married because the Second Empire told her to, and replied to his " Courage, Eugènie," simply : " I think I shall not catch cold ! " and went away in an army limber, with Placide stalking behind.

*　　*　　*　　*

LA GALETTE

Madeleine watched them go. Alone of all those present she, perhaps, noticed the change which seemed to settle down on the house, almost at once. It was not yet abandoned, but its women, its natural guardians, had gone from it.

The orderly, ration " fag " in mouth, cleared the table with a clatter, spilling grease on the floor. The marble overmantel, between the vases a former D'Archeville had brought from the sack of Pekin, and the Sèvres clock, became, as though by magic, littered with pipes, ashes, revolver ammunition, maps, indelible pencils—all the flotsam of men campaigning far from the decencies of property and housewifery. She tried to get the Baron on one side, having not for a moment forgotten her business at the château, but he was busy giving the Colonel, and a young officer who had come quietly in, as if by chance, some detail of the district. Before she could make her wants known, the Colonel, who had swept back the cloth, silver salts, plates, flower vases, all at one sweep, planted his 1 in 40,000 army map, and had his finger on the square pasture, and centreless E of building labelled " Ferme l'éspagnole " —the Spanish Farm.

" That belongs to mademoiselle," the interpreter interposed, prompted by the Baron, indicating her.

" Arthur," said the Colonel to the young officer, " your platoon can make a ' strong point ' there, where the roads join, and sleep in the house, while it's worth it ! "

In an instant, Madeleine relinquished all thoughts of pursuing her father on the Baron's bicycle. It was not merely that if she had had to choose between loyalty to her father and loyalty to the home, she would have chosen the latter. It was also that, had her father been there to counsel her, he would certainly have said, " Gardez la maison, ma fille ! " " Stick to the house, my girl."

" I'll go with you," she told the lieutenant, and went out into the darkness with him.

The horizon, from beyond Ypres, to the northeast, right round to near Béthune to the south, was ablaze. Over captured Merville, Estaires, Armentières, hung floating lights. The bombardment had ceased, the Bosche being too fearful of hitting their own advanced parties. The machine gun clamour was subsiding, both sides no longer knowing in the darkness where their bullets went. The farm Madeleine found already occupied. Tall lean figures, magnified in the candle-light, had stripped lengths of fabric from an aeroplane that had come down in the pasture, and lay half buried, grotesquely mangled, a putrefying mass of charred human flesh, wood and delicate machinery in the middle. They were covering every crevice in the kitchen windows. They made shelters, and gun-pits, and loopholes. By midnight the house was no

longer a farm, it was a tactical " strong point."
Madeleine had too much sense to protest, and
declined firmly to be evacuated. Calling the
officer and sergeant together, she pointed to her
door :

" This my room. I lock the door. See,
diggers ? "

" All serene, missy, sleep well," was the reply.

Madeleine did so. Like all those strong
enough to stand it, she felt a kind of exaltation
rising above any fear. Many a man felt like her
that night. The long-distance bombardment,
under which a human being was matched against
a lump of steel as large and many times harder
than himself, was over. To it succeeded the
direct struggle of man against man, with machine
gun, rifle and grenade. The Bosche were no
longer awe-inspiring once they got beyond the
range of their big guns. Let them come, the
sooner the better. The great offensive had been
threatened for months. It was here. Some
would survive it. Meantime the chances were
even. Madeleine slept.

*   *   *   *

No one knows, to this day, why the Bosche
never got to Hondebecq, but they halted a mile
short of it. Nothing happened. Anticlimax
ruled. War moods of exaltation, begotten of
danger, and the vitality that rises to meet it, cannot last. The battle of Bailleul dwindled out in

grey, cold spring weather. The trench line stiffened and became as fixed as the old line from the Ypres salient to La Bassée had been, before Messines and Paschendaele. The Bosche tried again and again farther south with no more effect. In the north the reorganized English line held good. The mood which came with this new state of things began to show itself, in civilians and soldiers alike, to be one of steady exasperation. For what did all this endless effort amount to ? One lived in a state not comparable to that of Peace, as regards comfort, business, or personal liberty. One side or the other made an offensive. The discomfort increased, the hectic war-time business was dislocated, personal liberty disappeared. But one thing remained— War. Enormously expensive, omnipresent, exasperating. Civilians and soldiers, the latter nearly all unwilling civilians now, felt its exasperation. Madeleine felt it. The Baron felt it. The troops billeted in the château and the farm felt it. The Baron, relieved from his wife's querulous exactions, Madeleine, set free from dutiful if doubtful belief in her father's methods of business, found the first Australian troops, if not charming visitors, at least good companions for the work in hand.

When it became certain that the enemy could get no farther, they were relieved, first by French troops, then by a Clydeside labour battalion. The Baron found his salle-à-manger filled with officers, who, though not actively ill-behaved, and probably well-meaning, he could see, whether he spoke their language or not, came of no particular family.

Madeleine found herself confronted with a set of cooks and quartermasters as businesslike as herself, far more akin to her in methods and outlook than had ever been the original volunteer army of England—who had paid what she asked with shy good humour. The neat walks and formal " bosquets " of the château garden, box-hedged, and decorated with plaster figures of nymphs and cupids, situate amid greenish pools, became pitted with latrines, and scarred with dugouts.

The village was beyond bullet range, but a 5.9 shell crashed in the top of the " shot " tower in the yard of the Spanish Farm. But worse than these evils were the continual thefts from the cellar of the château of wine, coal, and mattresses (for half the village had readily obtained leave to store their possessions there). At the farm, Madeleine was amazed to find herself forced to sell beer and butter, at less than cost price, by well-organized " strikes " that threatened to leave her merchandise on her hands.

The Baron, moreover, like so many of his age and nation at that time, had his private sorrow. Sharing his meals with the ever-changing messes of officers that filled his salle-à-manger (for the village being evacuated, there were no shops, and he was glad enough to trade away the accommodation he could to provide for food), he would stare round the youthful, unwarlike faces about him, faces of professional or business men, farmers or engineers from all corners of Great Britain or the Colonies, and would mutter, " I have no longer my son ! "

Madeleine, more self-controlled, wore black. No funeral service had been said for Jerome Vanderlynden. He had "disappeared" in the trite phrase of the Casualty Lists. The old church in the " place " of Hondebecq had three gaping shell-holes in the roof. The doors were closed, and it was declared in brief official notice " Unsafe." She did not even know if her numerous cousins and relations by marriage, scattered by the evacuation all across France from Evreux to Bordeaux, had heard what had happened to him. Nor did the thought of them greatly trouble her, accustomed to think and act for herself. She was doing what she knew so well her father was expecting of her. She was looking after the farm. The crops were sown. Such beasts as remained were tended. Jerome Vanderlynden had disappeared ! That could not be helped, any more than the thefts of all the fowls from the yard. Madeleine just went on.

*   *   *   *

The days went by, and the two civilians left in Hondebecq hardly noticed a change that came over things in the last week of July, 1918. That war, continuing year in and year out, could not be measured according to its " victories " of one side or the other, by people so intensely intimate with it, because they lived on the edge of the trenches. The most perhaps that they noticed was the gradual cessation of the shelling. It was no longer necessary to run to dugouts from one's bed at dawn, or from one's evening meal. Yet, at last, something really had happened. Madeleine was dimly conscious of a new atmosphere in the shuttered and sand-bagged salle-à-manger, when she went up on one of her usual errands to the château. The old interpreter, Mercadet, attached to the area, was sticking flags in the map of the Western Front, with his melancholy precision. " One has still some force left ! " he announced, and Madeleine saw without heeding that he was *moving the flags forward, instead of back*. It was, of course, Mangin's flank attack of July, the turning-point of the war. She paid more attention, however, a week or two later, when the troops in the farm began to move. The Bosche were gone from Kemmel Hill, was all they said. She lost touch with the war at this point, having no one to give her news.

She contrived to secure a couple of mules she found wandering about, and being handy with animals, shut them up and fed them sparingly. Probably nothing in the whole war frightened her so much as those weeks of the month of

September, when she was quite alone. Even the dog had been killed by the shell on the " shot " tower. Then, as the troops abandoned the château she found there a couple of aged veterans, left as billet wardens, and induced them, by pointing out truthfully how much better they would fare with her than in the Baron's company in the lonely château, to move to the farm. These two old casual labourers, who had enlisted in 1914 when drunk or workless, and had ever since been living better than before the war, made no difficulties. But it was no object to her to make hardships for the Baron, once she had gained her point, and secured potential guardians and labourers for the farm. She invited him to take his meals with her, and neither laughed nor chided as he stumped off, cigar glowing in the dark, to sleep on the moth-eaten rugs in his gun-room, revolver beside him, lest the château should be robbed—though what indeed there remained to steal in the darkened rooms, save the heavy furniture, no one could have said—wine, food, bedding, small objects had gone one by one, for use, or as souvenirs. The silver had been buried by Mercadet in the garden. But the Baron slept in the empty château, by instinct.

He was not alone long.

There was an almost dramatic fitness about the Army's choice of his one companion. A red-headed Welshman, answering to the name of Jacobs, was posted there, as District Sanitary

Engineer. The glamour and intensity was gone from the war, and the situation was now one for Municipal Health Officers. The appointment was additionally fitting. For though adorned by the title of " doctor," and adorning the rank of Captain, Jacobs was by profession a Borough Sanitary Engineer, one of those species peculiar to Great Britain. In its dying stages, those who ran the war were at last learning to put men to the job they could do best.

* * * *

Such was the situation of what the French staff aptly called the " open town " of Hondebecq in the last weeks of the war. By daylight, the Spanish Farm was at work, Madeleine and her two veterans, with the two mules, getting in all the undamaged crops—for nearly a quarter of the total acreage of the farm was lost in trench and wire, dugout and shell-hole. Hardly a day passed but had its hair-breadth escape from buried " duds " or unexploded shell, or caved-in gun-pit. Madeleine worked because it was natural to her—because she had nothing else to do, possibly with some unconscious idea of dedication to her father's memory. At dusk, Jacobs and the Baron would arrive, on bicycles, the one having toured his area, which stretched from the line of evacuation that ran from the Belgian border, through Hazebrouck down to Aire—away to the maze of desultory trenches from which the English troops were slowly pushing the last German machine gunners. The Baron usually acted as his guide, and in Jacobs' company avoided otherwise certain arrest. Madeleine would just be finishing her evening meal with the veterans. Jacobs would produce a field message book in which he had noted the map reference of any unburied offence, human or otherwise, and at his order the old men would jog off with one of the tireless mules in a salvaged limber, two shovels, a tin of disinfectant, and a lantern clattering in the springless vehicle. Madeleine cleared the table and served dinner to Jacobs and the Baron, who would sit over it, drinking canteen whisky and discussing in English-French and French-English the submarine menace and surface drainage, by means of any daily papers they had gleaned during the day's wandering, and with the help of Madeleine's translation. By the time both were ready to return to their never-made " beds " in the château, the veterans would come clattering back, the mules going at an unearthly amble in the darkness, and all was ready for the morrow.

*　　*　　*　　*

The War had been full of surprises—had been one great catastrophic surprise, since its declaration, and had kept up its pyrotechnic suddenness of change through all its four years. But the change that extinguished it outdid all else in strangeness. Late in October, the inhabitants of the château and the farm had heard the familiar sound of twelve-inch shells falling in Dunkirk, and never dreamed that they were never to hear that sound again. All day the roads and rail had been busy with French and English troops. They had halted in and around Hondebecq and passed on. The inhabitants of the farm and the château little dreamed that no more were to pass that way. The days and nights became quieter and ever more strangely quiet. There was a continual tension of the ear to catch that familiar rat-tat-tat, swish, boom. No sound came. Then, early in grey November, Jacobs and the Baron returned earlier than usual from their eternal cycling tour. In all the cellars of Haze-brouck, in all the hastily contrived, already-forgotten " strong points " in the area, they had not found one unburied mule, one neglected latrine. Or Jacobs had forgotten to take map references, for both were excited. Instead, they bent over a day-old English paper, that pretended to have the terms of the Armistice.

At first it was mere meaningless words. Nothing happened. The daily life of Hondebecq did not change. But soon a phenomenon was observed. Up the solid grey pavé road that Napoleon built from Lille to Dunkirk, along which the victorious armies of mid-October had advanced, there flowed, in the opposite direction, another human stream. No army this, and noth-

ing victorious about it, though here and there
a dirty old hat, or wonderfully made, decrepit
wheelbarrow was decorated with the flags of the
Allies, bought from Germans who had been sell-
ing them during their last weeks in the French
industrial area. By one and two, here a family,
there an individual with a dog, all those civilians
who had been swept within the German lines in
the offensives of 1914 or 1918, were walking
home. Such a home-coming surely never was
since misery began. Doré used to picture such
events in his illustrations to the Bible, but no one
has even seen the like in reality. For censors
had been strict, and the line of trenches where the
Allies had fronted the Germans unpassable.
Many a man of the Flemish border, or the Somme
downs, had hoped to find his house or his field
spared, and had to go to look himself in order to
be finally disillusioned. Madeleine, superintend-
ing the cleaning of the fields, the weed burning,
and autumn ploughing, saw them come in-
curiously, not able to realize that even she, who
had seen the whole War through, with the
trenches only just beyond the sight of her eyes
and never out of her hearing, had only now to
begin to learn what it really had been.

She left the veterans and the mules, busy in the
fields, and stood, for a few moments, on the edge
of the pavé, where the by-road to the farm left it,
watching the melancholy procession. True, some
were laughing, or greeted her with a cheer, but

the general impression of those pinched faces and anxious eyes, above worn and filthy clothes, gave a better idea than any historian will ever do, of the rigours of the blockade. Madeleine gained from the sight just her first inkling of the irreparable LOSS, that was to weigh upon the lifetime of her generation. War, the Leviathan, was giving up that which it had swallowed, but there was no biblical jubilation in them, none of those sharp terrors that, in scripture, foretell everlasting joy. Madeleine, better than any Bible-reading Protestant, comprehended. These poor souls (as she called them to herself, pityingly, for they had been " caught out," a defect she did not admit) had now got to work to catch up the wastage. A bright chance for most of them!

She returned to the farm, and now, finally convinced of the Armistice, yoked the mules to the strongest tackle she could find amid the abandoned and salvaged engineer stores that Jacobs had gathered, and began to pull away the barbed wire that laced the farm about, fifty yards at a time.

* * * *

She worked thus with the veterans, beating, shouting at, jerking the mouths of the mules, tugging, cutting, coiling the rusted venomous strands, piling the stout pickets on one side for further use, until it was nearly dark. Hastening home to prepare supper she noticed a dark bent

215

figure standing irresolutely in the courtyard.
She was walking over the slippery furrows by aid
of a half pick-handle, but, though thus armed, was
unafraid, and found something unaccountably
familiar in that listless bent-shouldered form.
Coming up to it, she gave a cry. It was the
ghost of Jerome Vanderlynden. She took him
by the hand, called him " Father," told him with a
choke in her voice that she was glad to see him
back. He just stared at her, but when spoken
to with decision, sat in the settle by the stove, and
smiled at the warmth and the smell of food.
Other sign of animation he would not give, nor
could she elicit what he thought, or how he had
found his way home. When her veterans came
in from the stable, she introduced him, and they
displayed all the kindliness of their sort, seemed
to understand at a glance the nature of the case,
called him " Poor old gentleman " and offered
him a ration cigarette, which he took, and immediately laid aside, as if he did not know its use.
He appeared better for the food and rest, and was
willing to be led to the bare tiled bedroom in
which he had always occupied the crazy old
double bed, where his children had been born and
his wife had died, and which, with the big old
press, two pegs, and two photos of the children,
constituted the whole furniture. He allowed
Madeleine to help him off with his sodden, shape-
less boots, rolled on the bed, and slept. Madeleine covered him and left him. In the morning

he appeared, awakened apparently by habit, or the smell of food, but replied only by vacant looks to his daughter's questions—pertinently designed as they were—" What has happened to the horse and tumbril ? " " Where have you been ? " " Do you remember me ? "

To the blandishments of the veterans (well-meant attempts to cheer him up), he paid no regard. It was not Jerome Vanderlynden who had returned. It was his ghost, something that, having lost its human mortal life, could not quite die, but must wander about the scenes to which it was accustomed, handle the objects it had used, but nothing more.

*   *   *   *

The condition of her father might have weighed heavily on Madeleine's mind had it been her only preoccupation, but fortunately it was not. First of all there was work. She was working harder than anybody ever works in England. From before the grey wet winter dawn, until long after the solitary army candle had been lighted in the kitchen, making grotesque shadows in the broken glass of the oriel window, her hands were never still, tugging, smoothing, shifting earth, timber, wire, weeds, produce ; housework, cooking, mending, were relaxations. Her mind and voice, thinking for and directing the veterans, the mules, presently the four bullocks and two milch cows, she contrived to obtain from those

217

wandering loose after the break-up of the trench lines, were never still except during the six or so hours that she slept. She regarded the Armistice as a piece of personal good luck. She would get the ground into some sort of order before the spring sowing. There would be manure, too, now that she had beasts, and with manure at hand, no Fleming ever quite loses heart. But besides work, the Peace that had so suddenly descended upon earth (without, alas, bringing that Goodwill supposed for centuries to accompany it) proved itself more inexorable than War.

Things began to move, released from the numbing strangulation of four and a quarter years. Jacobs and the veterans got orders to proceed to Courtrai, and continue the good work of cleansing the ornamental waters of that town from the use to which the German officers had put them. This disturbance of her source of labour gave Madeleine some moments' thought, but the sight of the Dequidt family, trudging back to their farm on foot, having been returned from evacuation in the Cherbourg district, opened up a new means of dealing with the problem. Her farm was nearly in order, her house more or less intact, her larder stocked with the good tinned stuff of the British Expeditionary Force Canteen. Theirs would not be so. She would give of her ample store, in return for work. There was one duty with which, however, she preferred to trust the two veterans, rather than any of her neighbours. Now that they were going, she thought of them in the terms in which she had once thought of a lieutenant called Skene. They were willing and well behaved. Moreover, they were going back to England (indicated by their saying to her, "What Ho, for Blighty," many times a day), so that they were safe. With smiles and encouraging words she led them to the foot of the shot tower. It was badly cracked by the shell that had hit the top, and great lumps of brickwork, a yard cube, had fallen, blocking the door ; elm beams a foot square lay jammed across the broken floor. It took three hours' hard work to effect an entrance. Then Madeleine kneeled down, put her arms through the broken boards, and fished up a length of stout iron chain. "Pull," she commanded, handing it over. The veterans, spitting on their hands, and setting their heels against the cobbles, called "Heave-ho !" as the chain emerged link by link. Finally, with a clatter and smash, a great iron box was retrieved. Madeleine unhooked it from the chain and bade them carry it to the house.

Once she had it on the kitchen table, having wiped the worst of the muddy water from it, and assured herself it was intact, she gave a sigh of relief. It was the savings of her father's lifetime, that had been withdrawn from the Savings Bank when Hazebrouck was first bombarded, and hidden thus by her. Seeing it before her, Madeleine made what the French call a "gesture"

—one of those actions prompted by emotions deeper than reason—in this case by the only genuine feeling at the base of the otherwise politician-manufactured Entente Cordiale. She had found the English friends in need, not too exacting, fairly ready to pay for what they wanted. They had been a comfort at the beginning of, through the long length of, and now at the daily growing aftermath of disillusionment with, the War. She took two notes, 20 francs each, from her purse, and distributed them to the veterans. Those members of England's Last Hope pocketed the money, exclaiming with one voice, "Thank you, Maddam," winking solemnly at each other.

That evening Jacobs took his leave, and she charged him for exactly what he had had. He departed into the darkness, to catch the newly established train service over the hastily repaired line, the veterans wheeling his valise and their own packs on a salved Lewis-gun hand cart.

*　　　*　　　*　　　*

With the departure of that party the British Army in Flanders finally left the Spanish Farm, after four years. The longed-for golden reign of Peace was re-established. And anything less golden cannot be imagined. Madeleine lost no time in getting into touch with the evacuated neighbours now returning to their farms. They were nearly all women, and though they were willing enough to work, they had neither the dexterity nor the resources of the British Army. Madeleine wished indeed, before many weeks were over, that the War had lasted longer. There was the big kitchen window, not to mention sundry other panes broken by carelessness, or by concussion of bombing and shelling, to be reglazed. There were leaks in the roof to mend, there was the shot tower to rebuild—unless indeed she built some other stowage room for all the things it used to hold—sacks, " fertilizer," tools, roots, grain, hops, spare cart covers, timber. There were nineteen gates missing, endless lengths of hedge and ditch practically to be made over again. The hurdles were all gone, and worst of all, the great fifteen-feet hop-poles and stout wire. As was usual throughout French Flanders, the British Army had burned every piece of wood upon the farm. Madeleine did not blame them. A French or any other army would have done the same. There was, however, one good job that the War had done : the tall elms round the pasture had been completely barked by the numerous mounted units that had succeeded each other. They would die, and the proprietor (the Baron, to wit) would do well to sell them at once, while the price was so high. The ground would be disencumbered, more grass would grow and the great roots would no longer suck up all the manure one

put down. The only loser would be the Baron.
It was his affair.

* * * *

For already Peace had brought that endless
attempt to go one better than one's neighbour,
which, for four years, had been hidden under the
more immediate necessity to go one better than
the Bosche. Thus Madeleine, perceiving that
whatever the eventual scheme of compensation, she
must pay, in the first instance, nearly all the loss
occasioned, began actually to grudge the English
their demobilization. Had they (and their dumps
of material) remained in the neighbourhood, she
would have got them to do plumbing and glazing,
ditching and joinery, and to give her good telephone wire, aeroplane canvas, oil, paint and nails.
Instead of which, every day that she went as far as
the Lille road, she saw trainloads of useful English, singing and cheering on their way to Dunkirk, where they were being demobbed by
thousands a day. So she grew bitter, and having
no one else to blame (for who could blame
old Jerome, wandering helpless like a worn-out
horse) she began to blame the English for going
away. Madame la Baronne had returned to the
château. Placide was once more functioning, and
the Baron was only seen at the farm on his walks,
as before the offensive of 1918. So that there
was absolutely no one but the English to blame for
having departed so inopportunely. There was

nothing exceptional in Madeleine's case. It was, indeed, the common feeling in all those French and Flemish farms on the border of what had been the trenches (the frontiers of civilization) and was now the Devastated Area (something no one wanted, and everybody was tired of hearing about). This being so, the Government, depending upon votes, saw that something must be done to retain those sources of its power and emoluments, lest they be filched by Bolsheviks, Germans, Socialists or other enemies—in fact by persons who might come to wield the power, and enjoy the resulting advantages, which every government looks upon as the permanent reward of the endless corruption by which it has maintained itself.

Thus, about this time, Madeleine began to hear of things called " Reparations," that the Germans were going to be made to pay. She was invited to inscribe at the Mairie the list of damage done by the War to the farm. She went to see Monsieur Blanquart, and furnished him with a list that totalled 131,415 francs 41 centimes (the total market value of the farm in 1914 being about 120,000 francs). Monsieur Blanquart inscribed the lot. He did more. Like every one else, he felt that he had had an atrocious time for many years, and that nothing was too good for him. Keeping in close touch with his daughter Cécile, at Amiens, he had been quite sharp enough to see how things were shaping.

He had hung in the windows of his little parlour, and all round the mayoral office at the Estaminet de la Mairie, in place of the patriotic appeals by M. Deschanel to fortitude and patience, in place of lists of conscripts, and of ever-mounting food prices, little cards inscribed "Blanquart, financial agent"; "Blanquart, bonds, shares, assurances." He unfolded golden schemes to Madeleine, who listened with her special "stupid peasant" expression that she kept for the occasions when she was thinking hard. Her list of war damages was based not so much on facts and figures as on her one idea of any monetary transaction—namely, to ask twice as much as a thing is worth, in the certainty that you will be beaten down by at least a quarter. She was no more deceived by the talk in the papers than by Blanquart's "financial operations." She knew how difficult it was for her to part with money or money's worth, and judged the Germans, and Blanquart's stocks and shares, by her own standards. Pay ! Not likely, Germans or Royal Dutch, not if they could help it. But standing hatless and vacant-faced before Blanquart, she was working out in her mind one of her slowly conceived plans, so much less simple than one would have supposed from her appearance. She had enough cash in the iron box to buy two horses and get along until harvest.

"Look here, Monsieur Blanquart, I'll take 50,000 francs' worth of your bonds, and pay you when I get my ' Reparations.' "

But Blanquart had not lived in the village all those years for nothing. " You comprehend," he replied, " your reparations are subject to discussion ! "

" No doubt; but I suppose one will pay us something ! "

" Undoubtedly, but how much ?—that's the point ! "

Madeleine got up and moved toward the door. " Oh, well, it's a pity ! " she said.

Blanquart hated to see her go. She was one of the richest " heiresses " in the village (as heiresses go in France), and there was only Marie to divide it with her when old Jerome died. Moreover, she had quite a reputation for the part she had played in the last phases of the War, and it would be a great help to be able to say to the others : " Madeleine Vanderlynden has taken 50,000." He offered : " Look here, I'll buy your reparations for 40,000 ! "

" No, nothing to be done," was the answer, hand on the latch.

In his heart Monsieur Blanquart pested the sacred peasants. But something must be arranged. " Very well, I sell you 40,000 worth of securities, and you can pay me when you get your ' Reparations ' ! "

Madeleine left the doorway and came back to the table. Looking through his stocked portfolio she chose only bearer bonds (coupons appealed to her ; the less tangible dividend warrant of inscribed or registered stock did not), some national, some industrial, some lottery. Thus armed, she returned to the farm.

*   *   *   *

Thus came what Politicians called " Peace," but mostly French people, realists in a sense that the English public never is, spoke of it as the " era of La Galette "—the cake which one could eat and yet have again, the pie in which every one's finger might be—the lucky-bag into which all might dip.

Upon the mentality of France, with its dominant peasant outlook, only one deep impression was made. The Germans were beaten. Therefore their money could be got at. Anyone who did not get at it was a fool, simply. This was not piracy. The Germans had invited a contest, and lost. The loser pays—that is logic as well as human nature. When the first hints were dropped that there might be delays, even a dwindling of the golden stream that was to flow from Berlin—public feeling became so strong that Government had hastily to vote sums " on account of " the Reparations to be exacted. In every village, men, and more often women, asked each other : " What have you estimated your damages at ? "   " What have you received on account ? "   In place of the War-time watchwords " La Patrie est en danger " and " On les aura," there might very reasonably have been dis-

played another : " La Galette "—The Cake that
every one might take. "L'assiette au beurre "—
The butter-dish to grease every itching palm. "Le
pot au vin "—The loving-cup that was ever full.

*   *   *   *

Before she could put the War finally away from
her, Madeleine had to go through a process which
might be called in English, the laying of ghosts.
Without active belief in the supernatural, and
prone to laughter at those who dared not pass the
Kruysabel, after dusk, without crossing themselves (this superstition was one of the safeguards
that had kept her meetings with Georges secure),
she preserved to the full the clear feeling of all
primitives, that the Living are connected with,
influenced by, the Departed. The most immediate case was that of her father. Jerome Vanderlynden had never recovered his reason, but
had recaptured a few words, and most of his
bodily functions. What had been done, or not
done, to him, during his eight months behind the
German lines, will never be known. A neighbour, also swallowed up by the swift invasion of
April, 1918, had seen him, near Lille, working in
a field, under German direction, but had not been
recognized. At that date, even, the old man had
lost his senses. He bore no particular signs of
ill-usage, other than the common starvation
caused by blockade, and, after weeks of loving
care, Madeleine, nearest to him, most like him

of all people on earth, managed to make out what
he mumbled to himself, with that scared look,
when his food was set before him : " There's
nothing left to eat ! " he whispered, with a frightened glance around. Then, when coaxed, he
would eat, rapidly, defensively.

Madeleine, no theorist, came to the conclusion
that the fact that he had been interrupted in the
middle of sowing his potatoes, and had then found
the stock of food at Marie's farm destroyed or
taken, had unhinged his mind. At that she had
to leave it, and although the old man's iron health
did not vary, she had sorrowfully to admit that,
as father and parent, as companion and guide, he
was gone from her, just as effectively as though
she had buried him in the churchyard, beneath
the battered, spireless old church, that filled all
one side of the grande place of the village. So
strongly did she feel this, that she refused to let
the curé worry him about his soul.

Thus was one ghost laid.

*   *   *   *

There was another ghost, one that haunted her
with no material presence, did not inhabit the
farm, but hovered, a dim grey figure at the back
of her mind.

About Christmas, 1918, in the dead slack of
the year, when most of the clearing of the land
was done, when the autumn sowing was over and
it was too early for the spring one, she had leisure

to go up to the Kruysabel. She had neglected this ceremony since the invasion of 1918, chiefly because the disappearance of her father had left the whole weight of the farm on her shoulders, partly because, steadfast as she was, she changed as must every living thing, and Georges was receding from her, with the past. She knew that the place had been fortified into a " strong point," and had she not known, she would have guessed from the fact that the wooden-gate was gone, and the alley that led up the hill, beaten into pulp by military traffic. She scrambled up among the undergrowth, untouched save for shell-holes, and a few places where the vegetation had fired, or hung grey and sickly, reeking of gas. This made her frown and put on her expression as of one about to smack a naughty child. At the top, treading some barbed wire, she came out into the little clearing, leapt a half-decayed trench, and stood by the hunting shelter. Outwardly it was not much changed. A woman, looking at it with the eyes of Madeleine, could see that it was no longer the same place, although its greeny-grey woodland colour, and shape that blurred into the surrounding undergrowth, had been carefully preserved, so that it was probably imperceptible to the best glasses a few hundred yards away. The door was undone, and she pushed it open, stood and gasped. Nothing in the previous four years and a half had quite prepared her for what she found. The place had been skilfully gutted.

229

Not only the glass from the windows, the whole of
the rugs, cushions, seats, and fittings were gone,
but the actual partitions had been removed, leaving the brick chimney-piece alone supporting an
empty shell. The trap of the cellar had been
forced, and in the aperture left was a steel and
concrete " pill-box," its machine gun embrasures
level with the window-sills. At the opposite end,
just where there had stood the divan on which she
had held Georges in her arms, the floor had been
torn up, the earth dug away, to make room for a
similar erection. The only recognizable remains
of the furniture were some of the animal heads
and photographs of hunting groups, all adorned
with moustaches or other attributes, obscene or
merely grotesque, in army indelible pencil, or
fastened with field telephone wire. It took
Madeleine's plodding mind a moment to size it
all up, from the gas-gong hanging from a nail,
to the painted wooden notice-board, in English :
" Any person found using this Strong Point as
a latrine will be severely dealt with. C.R.E.
Defence lines."

Then she let the door swing to, turned her back
on the place, and walked away. It was not in her
to philosophize. What had been done, she felt
like a personal injury. If the place had merely
been dirtied and damaged by billeting or shell-
fire, she would have shrugged her shoulders and
put it straight. But this systematic conversion
struck deep at her sense of personal possession.

They had challenged her right to something she felt to be most deeply her own. For once she was at a loss, was done, beaten, did not know how to adjust herself, hit back. Georges seemed smaller, further off, than she had ever felt him. Her love for him now seemed almost ridiculous, temporary, and for ever done with. She was aroused from her reverie by the thick undergrowth that barred her steps, and realized that she was walking down the north-eastern slope of the wood, with her back to the farm. That recalled her to herself. She retraced her steps, skirted the clearing, dodged the trenches and wire, and descended the hill towards home, head up, face impenetrable, mistress of herself. But in her heart she was banking up the slow burning fires of resentment. The less easy it was to find legitimate fuel for them, the more she fed them with the first thing or person that came to hand, feeling herself wronged and slighted by all the world.

*   *   *   *

There remained one more ghost to be laid, one thin wraith that Madeleine hardly noticed, hovering at the back of her war-memories. She did not call up this last apparition, it came to her.

As grey January slid into February, she became aware, amid her engrossing preoccupation with the farm, that a Labour Corps battalion was working on the clearance of the neighbouring trench-lines. They were composed of German prisoners and Chinese, officered by a few English. Presently an orderly called, a German orderly, sent to buy eggs. She sent him about his business, curtly. This brought an officer, fair, bald, thickset, speaking little French. He smiled at her with an irritating cocksureness, and inquired for her father. Then she recognized him. It was the Lieutenant Millgate who had come to the farm late one night in 1915 with Lieutenant Skene, to join the Easthamptons. She found him some eggs for old times' sake, charged him a pre-war price and forgot him again. He was no ghost ; he was an insignificant fact, and did not haunt her.

But there came a grey day when he reappeared, and not alone. Another officer in khaki, taller but slighter, was riding behind him, and tried to greet old Jerome, who ignored the greeting. Before she knew what had happened, Geoffrey Skene stood before her. Almost mechanically, for she could not say what she felt, she bade him enter and sit down. Once he was seated, following her with his eyes, all her vindictiveness found vent in the words :

" Will you have some coffee ? The Allies stole all our wine ! " Then she softened again, and gave him good coffee, because, like all women, she had a tender spot somewhere for a man who had once desired her. But it was only for a moment. He sat there, unaltered, just as he had

sat when she had sent him to deliver a message
to Georges. And the thought that Georges had
gone out of her life, and that this lesser man of
hers was on his way to England, to go out of her
life just as effectually, hurt her possessive and
domineering instincts. She said bitterly, " I lost
my fiancé, after all ! " and as he murmured some
condolence her spleen overcame her, and she
lashed out with her tongue at all the damage done
to the farm and to her father, the destruction of
her brothers and Georges, at all the work there
was to do, and no one to do it.

She saw Millgate fidget, heard him say in
English, " Come on ! " Then she saw Skene
rise, bid her good-bye, and go. She moved to
the door, but for the life of her she could not say
if she wanted him to go or stay.

Then, as he swung his leg, in its soiled army
clothes, over his horse's back, straightened up,
and clattered away, she knew. She did not want
him, had never wanted him, nor any Englishman,
nor anything English. He was just one of the
things the War, the cursed War, had brought on
her, and now it, and they, were going. Good
riddance. Nor was her feeling unreasonable.
The only thing she and Skene had in common,
was the War. The War removed, they had
absolutely no means of contact. Their case was
not isolated. It was national.

* * * *

233

THE SPANISH FARM

So Madeleine remained in the Spanish Farm, and saw no more English, for the Labour Corps soon broke up and went, and she did not care. She was engrossed in one thing only : to get back, sou by sou, everything that had been lost or destroyed, plundered or shattered, by friend or foe, and pay herself for everything she had suffered and dared. And as there was a Madeleine more or less, widowed and childless, bereaved and soured, in every farm in north-eastern France, she became a portent. Statesmen feared or wondered at her, schemers and the new business men served her and themselves through her, while philosophers shuddered. For she was the Spanish Farm, the implacable spirit of that borderland so often fought over, never really conquered. She was that spirit that forgets nothing and forgives nothing, but maintains itself, amid all disasters, and necessarily. For she was perhaps the most concrete expression of humanity's instinctive survival in spite of its own perversity and ignorance. There must she stand, slow-burning revenge incarnate, until a better, gentler time.

Printed in Great Britain
Butler & Tanner Ltd.,
Frome and London

CPSIA information can be obtained
at www.ICGtesting.com
Printed in the USA
BVHW081200190223
658756BV00002B/394